VENGEANCE
REQUIRED

ALISA A. MURRAY

ONE

Normally, Ovasta Kaiser was awakened by the feel of wet drool from her German shepherd, Major, gently stroking her hand with his tongue. Today, she opened her eyes to the darkness of the night, hearing only the rustling of leaves blowing outside of her bedroom window. She glanced at the alarm clock on the nightstand next to her bed. *5:00 a.m.* Groggy, she got out of bed and stumbled into the bathroom to shower before work. She always enjoyed the warm pulsating water running down her body, releasing tension from the muscles in her neck, shoulders, and arms.

She needed relaxation now more than ever. The hospital board of directors was going to vote on whether she or her colleague, Phillip Michaels, would be the next president. Several candidates who were nominated had been eliminated in the initial vote leaving only her and Michaels. Ovasta felt as equally qualified as Michaels, if not more. But he had long-term relationships with more board members. Ovasta's real saving grace was that the retiring board president Stephen Gerard recommended her as his successor.

Gerard was ill and decided to step down from his position to focus on his recovery. Still, Ovasta knew the vote could go either way.

A noise at the bathroom door snapped her from her thoughts. She wrapped a towel around herself, sliding out of the tempered glass shower door. A smile donned her face as she peeped into the room. It was Major. Sitting. Leash in his mouth and ears erect, he wagged his tail. Ovasta rubbed the top of his brown, domed-shaped head, gave him a hug, and took the leash from his mouth. "Okay, boy, I'll let you out so you can use it." Major trailed her to the back door, running out when she opened it. "I won't be taking you for a walk this morning," she shouted after him. "I want to get to work early today."

Since he was potty trained, Major always went to the same area outside behind his doghouse. Afterwards, he ran back in the house and ate his breakfast.

Ovasta went into her room and put on her favorite black skirt suit which she thought perfectly accentuated her slender five-foot-ten-inch frame. She decided to wear her Prada shoes, a gift she received for Christmas last year.

Since the forecast called for no inclement weather, she opted to take Major back outside with a bowl of dog food and water and place it inside his house. Major was full and would wait several hours before eating again. Ovasta rubbed him on the head and left for work.

Ovasta casually pulled into the underground hospital parking lot. Although nervous, she'd never let it show. She got out of her black Audi and rode the parking lot elevator to the second floor. As soon as she walked out, there was her longtime friend, Riya Davison, whom she'd known since grade school. They attended the same medical school as both wanted to become nurses. Midway through college, however, Ovasta changed her mind and decided to work in hospital administration, additionally majoring in clinical counseling. After getting her license, she got a job working for a behavioral health agency. When Riya got a job at the hospital, she saw there was an opening in the social work department. Immediately, she informed Ovasta about the position. Ovasta applied and was ultimately hired. Subsequently, heading the hospital's social work department within a few years' time.

"Hey, Vee, good morning." Riya still called her by the nickname she had given Ovasta when they were children and Riya couldn't pronounce her name correctly. Ovasta tried telling her repeatedly how to say it. *Oh voss ta!* Even after all these years, she sometimes wondered if Riya could properly pronounce it.

"Come on, let's go to my office and have a cup of coffee before we start our day," Ovasta suggested.

"You mean before *you* start *your* day. I've been here since five-thirty a.m. and have already had two cups. By the way, you look nice."

"Thanks, I'll be glad when this day is over. I'm tired of thinking about the vote. The suspense is killing me."

"Me, too," replied Riya, her doe-like eyes smiling at her best friend.

Ovasta walked down the hall and into her office,

followed by Riya who sat her petite five-foot-two-inch frame down in what she labeled "her chair." It was a red leather recliner situated in the middle of two Burberry wingbacks. In front of her, pictures of birds in flight donned the walls. Several of which Ovasta painted herself, a hobby she picked up a few years ago. Ovasta grabbed an OSU mug, her alma mater, out of a small wooden cabinet in the corner. "Be back in the minute," she said as hurried out of her office and down the hospital corridor.

Vince Parker strolled in a few minutes later while Riya was sitting in Ovasta's office.

"Good morning. How are you?" He spoke to Riya who slid up from her slouched position once he entered the room.

"Hey, I'm good. Thanks for asking. As always I'm waiting for Vee. She went to get some coffee. She'll be back in a minute."

Vince walked in the office giving his head a tiny nod. Sitting in the other wing back chair next to Riya. "I figured. It's the way she always starts her mornings."

When Ovasta returned, she stood in the doorway holding a cup of coffee, looking at Vince, the hospital's top neurosurgeon and her longtime love. The couple met four years ago at a medical convention. He lived in New York and she in Ohio. When offered a position at a hospital in Ohio, he jumped at the chance. It was a win-win situation —promotion *plus* close proximity to Ovasta. At six-foot-one, with wavy black hair, the chiseled facial features of Superman, and a muscular build, Vince was strikingly handsome even in scrubs. The hazelnut aroma began to fill the air around her. "What are you two talking about?" she questioned.

Vince laughed. "Why, you of course."

Riya rose out of the chair, fluffing the back of her curly, shoulder-length, reddish-brown hair. "I'd better go back to the nurse's station before they start paging me. See you lovebirds later." She blew a kiss at both of them. "Vee, call me as soon as you hear anything. You know I'm rooting for you."

"Thanks for the well wishes. I'll call you."

Vince stood up and waved goodbye and turned to Ovasta. "You're beautiful today as always and I especially like those shoes."

Ovasta chuckled. "Of course you like them. You were the one who gave them to me."

Vince smiled. "How could I have forgotten?" he questioned sarcastically while taking the coffee mug from her hands and placing it on her large oak desk. Gazing lovingly into her hazel-brown eyes, he ran his fingers through her coal-black, shoulder-length hair. Leaning forward he gave her a quick peck on the lips. "I came by to wish you luck."

"Thanks, it is going to be a close vote. I need all the luck I can get."

"Since the vote is not until two, why don't we go out to lunch around noon? That way you can at least have one relaxing moment during the day. Anyway, there are a few things I want to discuss with you."

Ovasta tilted her head to the right, squinting her eyes. She was trying to figure out why he wanted to go to lunch when her day was already extremely busy. "Can't it wait until after the vote?" she replied with mild irritation in her voice.

"*No*. You need to relax and I want to talk," Vince stated sternly, the smile fleeting from his face.

Ovasta sighed, blinking her eyes swiftly several times in a row. "Alright, then noon it is."

"So it's settled. I'll meet you here and we can ditch this place for about an hour and a half. We'll go someplace nice for lunch. I've got time. My next surgery isn't until three."

After giving Ovasta another peck on the lips, Vince left the office. Ovasta wondered why he insisted on going to lunch today, of all days. But she had to admit a little time spent away from the hospital was exactly what she needed. Vince was extremely perceptive and could always tell when she needed some time away from work. Ovasta smiled within herself. Vince always had her best interest at heart. It was one of the main reasons why she loved him so much.

Punctual as always, Vince was back in her office at 11:54 a.m. "Come on, honey, let's go." She glanced up at him from her desk. Vince changed from hospital scrubs into a tailored black suit and the tie she gave him for his birthday.

Although he always looked nice, she was surprised he was so well dressed in the middle of the day. Especially considering he had to change in a couple of hours for a late afternoon surgery. She pondered the more about what was going on, knowing that Vince always had something up his sleeve. Whatever the case, she decided to let those feelings pass her by.

She smiled at him and said, "You look nice. I especially like the tie."

"Of course you do," he laughed. "You're the one who bought it."

"How could I have forgotten?" she replied mocking their previous conversation."

"Oh, come on, let's get out of here and get something to eat." He reached for her hand, rushing her out of the building.

Shortly after arriving at La Restaurant de la Garden, Vince whispered something to the maître d' who seated them immediately. Ovasta was very surprised at how hastily they were seated. Suspicion nagged at her.

"How did we get a table so fast?"

"I have connections," he winked with a wry smirk on his face. Vince eased out the chair and signaled for her to sit down, then he sat across from her and loosened the tie around his neck.

The table was near the window. The sunlight bathed Ovasta's face giving her a clear view of the landscape. The orange and brown leaves were falling from the nearby trees. In the far distance, she could see the lake which ebbed and flowed upon the distant shore ever so calmly.

"Beautiful, isn't it?" Vince's voice interrupted her thoughts.

"Yes, it is." Ovasta leisurely turned her head away from the window.

As soon as she did, she could see the servers coming with food. Placing petit fillet mignon with a baked potato and a salad in front of Vince and giving her salmon, rice pilaf, and a salad. Vince pulled the silverware out of the cloth napkin on the table then put the napkin across his lap. He gave Ovasta a broad smile, exposing most of his upper teeth. "I took the liberty of ordering our meals in advance so we can get back to the hospital in a timely fashion."

"Wait a minute. First, you take me to an expensive restaurant during the middle of the day when we both have to get back to work. Second, once we get here our table is ready as soon as we walk in the door, and now you are telling me you've already ordered our meals. What in the world is going on?" She questioned as her peering eyes scanned Vince's face.

"I've got a big surgery this afternoon and really need to eat. Can we just enjoy our food for a moment?" Vince had already cut his meat and was placing a bite in his mouth.

"Oh, all right. This salmon does look good." Ovasta placed the napkin in her lap and began eating.

Within a few minutes, Vince had finished all of his food while Ovasta had only eaten the salad but only a bit of salmon. She gazed up at Vince while pushing the plate away from her. "The food is good, but I'm really too nervous to eat it all. My stomach is full of butterflies."

"Don't worry. I believe that everything will work out fine. Anyway, you can always take it home. If you don't eat it, I'm sure Major would love some fish."

"He absolutely would!"

Vince snickered as he flagged down the waiter and asked for the check. It was quickly brought to the table. He cleared his throat, then looked directly into Ovasta's eyes. "Right before we began eating, you asked me what in the world was going on. Allow me to answer your question. It's you, Ovasta. You are my world. I'd like you to become my wife."

Vince stood up, walked over to her side of the table, and got down on one knee. He pulled a tiny box out of his suit jacket pocket, opened it, and lifted the box with a ring inside towards Ovasta. Staring into her face. His eyes shone like opal gemstones. "Will you marry me?" he questioned sweetly.

Ovasta laid her right hand across her chest to stop her heart from pounding. Her tear-filled eyes twinkled at Vince. *"Yes!"* she exclaimed with overwhelming glee.

Vince placed the ring on her finger. "This seals the deal," he whispered happily as he rose to his feet.

Applause and joy filled the room as he kissed her. At that moment, the crowd appeared to shrink. It seemed as if they were the only people there.

A stately gentleman, who appeared to be in his mid-seventies, came over to their table. "Congratulations!" he said in a British accent as he picked the bill up from off the table. He smiled at the pair focusing his gaze on Vince.

"I want to pay for your meal today. My wife and I recently celebrated forty years of marriage. She's the boss," he said pointing to Ovasta. "Remember that."

"I'll keep that in mind," chuckled Vince. "Thank you so much for your generosity."

"You know, I'm in total agreement with what he said," joked Ovasta as they headed out and got in the car to return to work.

"Oh, I have no doubt that you are." Vince looked at her while putting the key in the ignition. "Do you know why I wanted to propose today? Prior to the vote? It's because I wanted you to know I love you, board president or not."

"I see you put a lot of thought into this. However, I could never believe you proposed for any reason other than you love me and want us to spend the rest of our lives together."

Vince took his right hand off the steering wheel and gently caressed hers. "I certainly do."

The ride back to the hospital was pleasantly silent. Ovasta replayed the proposal repeatedly in her mind, staring at her magnificent diamond in awe. Every now and then Vince would glance at her with a loving smile that she'd return. Tickled with excitement, they hopped out of the car as soon as Vince pulled into a spot in the parking garage.

"I'll call you when I get out of surgery. You should know the results by then."

"I'm still feeling a bit edgy, but I think I can accomplish good things for the hospital whether I'm head of the board or not."

"That's my girl." Vince brushed his hand up and down

the small of her back as they rode the garage elevator to the main floor. He hugged her and headed to surgery.

She went straight to the nurse's station as she couldn't wait to tell Riya the good news. She had always wanted to marry Vince but was beginning to wonder if the feeling was mutual.

Ovasta glided down the hall like a runway model. Shoulders back, head erect. She could see Riya at the end of the corridor.

Riya started moving in Ovasta's direction and when she neared her, asked, "What's going on, Vee? You seem so excited. Did they take the vote already?" Riya's eyes broadened, her eyebrows elevated as Ovasta lifted up her left hand displaying the two-carat marquise diamond ring. Riya screeched. "Oh, my God! Did Vince propose?"

"Yes!" Ovasta extended her arms toward Riya who grabbed her, squeezing her tightly. "Even if I don't win the vote, this is still one of the happiest days of my life!"

"I am so happy for the two of you. I can't wait to start helping with the wedding plans," exclaimed Riya as she hugged Ovasta a second time.

Riya left to return to the nurse's station and Ovasta bounced happily to the boardroom to speak with several members one more time prior to the vote. Upon arrival, she saw her opponent, Phillip Michaels, whispering to another board member, Samuel King. Michaels was extremely well dressed in his expensive-looking navy suit which was tailored to fit his lanky six-foot frame. King, who was several inches shorter than Phillip, saw Ovasta coming and stopped speaking.

"Hey, Ovasta, we were just talking about you," remarked Phillip, glancing around once King had abruptly gotten quiet.

"I'm sure you were," she replied in a less-than-friendly tone.

Phillip chuckled, his brown eyes dancing in Gucci glasses. He extended his hand in order to shake hers. "May the best *man* win."

Ovasta held out her limp hand. As soon as Phillip saw the other board members entering the room, he quickly clutched her hand.

"Now that's what I like to see," commented board president Stephen Gerard on the handshake. "It doesn't matter who wins today. What matters is we all want what's best for this hospital and the patients we serve."

Gerard gestured for the board members, eight men and four women, to sit down at the oval-shaped English cherry conference table in the board room, then called the meeting to order. He was no longer plump due to his illness although he retained some girth around his waistline. His thinning hair had turned perfectly white within the past year. Although pale and sullen, he maintained a commanding presence. "We all know why this meeting was called and what needs to be done here today. I have served this hospital for many years and am no longer able to do so. I'm so thankful I was given this opportunity to serve. It was a painstaking decision, but I knew it was time to step down due to my failing health. However, I should like to say I am more than willing to assist the incoming president in any way possible." Gerard picked up the glass of water that was sitting in front of him. He drank from it gradually then cleared his throat. "Okay, enough with the preliminaries. I would like everyone to take a ballot and vote for who you believe will be the best person for the job. I'm sure each person here has been mulling over this very important decision. My secretary, Lindsay, is here to pass out the ballots. After you have picked your candidate, Lindsay will come back around with a box for you to place it in. When we're all done, I will open up the box in front of you and tally up the votes. Now let's do this."

Ovasta tried hard not to make direct eye contact with anyone, especially Phillip. However, she could see Gerard looking at her out of the corner of her eye. She glanced up at him and he gave her that reassuring half-smile she had grown to love over the past few years. By the time she turned away from him, Lindsay, freckle-faced and barely out of high school, was next to her with a ballot. She checked off her name and slid the ballot into the box. Lindsay pranced away and Ovasta leaned back in her chair with confidence. She fixed her gaze on Gerard who waited on Lindsay to return with the ballot box.

"Are we ready to hear the results?" questioned Gerard. No one responded. Lindsay handed Gerard the box. He poured out the thirteen ballots on the table, counting them deliberately. Phillip received the first four votes. Ovasta began to get understandably nervous and began rubbing the back of her neck, something she always did when she felt uneasy. What she thought would be a close decision was beginning to seem like a landslide. The next six votes, however, were in her favor. She breathed a sigh of relief knowing at least some of the board members supported her. Only three votes left. Two were for Phillip. They were now tied six to six with the deciding vote left on the table. Gerard opened the last ballot. Based upon his dismal expression, Ovasta was sure Phillip had won. She still decided this was one of the best days of her life. Gerard glanced up with dispatch at Ovasta and then Phillip. "Congratulations to Ovasta Kaiser, who has the deciding vote and is now the new president of the board for this hospital."

Ovasta could hardly believe it! She fought hard to hold back the tears of joy which began to stream down her face. She stood up to shake Phillip's hand but he swiftly got up from the table and exited the room, retrieving his cell phone from his pocket as he left. She saw him put the phone to his ear as he scurried away.

All the other board members remained in the boardroom. For a moment, she watched the door, expecting Phillip to return after he made his phone call, hoping he would at least come back into the room to shake her hand. *He'll come around*, she thought as the other board members rallied around to congratulate her. Once she began to converse with them, she soon forgot about Phillip.

Ovasta strolled out of the board room and nearly skipped down to her office. Within the next month, she'd be moving into Gerard's office. Ovasta had no problem waiting patiently for him to move his personal belongings and probably couldn't rush him out even if she wanted to. She did hope he'd let her have his photograph with former President George W. Bush. Or at least allow her to make a copy of it. Gerard was proud of the fact that he'd been invited to the White House in order to discuss Medicare reforms. With his help, the president's ten-year privatization options were created.

There was a lot of work to do and Ovasta hoped to have as much success as her predecessor. She was honored to have had a chance to work with such a highly-esteemed man. Hospital board presidents from across the nation came to meet him on a regular basis to discuss how he turned a troubled hospital into one which was thriving and well respected across the nation. In addition to the hospital, he was also involved with many charitable organizations as well as volunteering to serve food at the neighborhood soup kitchen whenever possible. The dignity, integrity, and innovative ideas he brought to the hospital could not be matched. She would miss him greatly but looked forward to receiving his sage advice.

Within a few moments of arriving in the office, her cell phone rang. She knew by the special ringtone it was Vince calling to find out what happened. "Hello," she answered, her voice almost purring.

"Well? What's the verdict?" he pleaded.

"I don't know how to tell you this, but Vince, you are engaged to the newly-elected board president!"

"Congratulations, baby, I am so proud of you. Have you told Riya yet?"

"No, I haven't had a chance to. I literally just walked back into my office when you called."

"Well, I know you can't wait to tell her. I will catch up with you in about two hours and we can all get something to eat if Riya is available."

"Okay, I'll see you then, bye."

Ovasta hung up the phone. It rang again. Riya. "I'm the new board president!" exclaimed Ovasta, not giving her a chance to say anything.

"Congrats, I'm so happy for you!"

"Thanks. It actually came down to the very last vote. Do you know when I won, Phillip refused to shake my hand. He literally ran out of the room to make a phone call, and never came back."

"Wow! That confirms what kind of man he really is. A thousand-dollar suit, zero character. A real man would have shaken your hand and offered his support. His behavior was childish and proves the board members made the right decision by making you president."

"Vince would like the three of us to go out tonight," Ovasta said, abruptly changing the subject.

"Are you sure he's okay with me coming? Sometimes I feel like the third wheel."

"Actually, it was his idea. See you in about two hours?"

"Yep, I'll be there."

Vince, Ovasta, and Riya met at Ovasta's waterfront townhouse around 6:00 p.m.

"Hey, guys, it's been a long day. I really don't feel like going out." Ovasta opened the door, sped across the room, and stretched face-up across her tan sofa still wearing her shoes and London Fog trench coat.

Vince stood over her, amused. "Okay, how about I call and have some Chinese food delivered because you look like you just surrendered to General Custer at the Battle of Little Big Horn."

"Really, didn't Custer get killed in that battle?" queried Riya sarcastically.

Vince shrugged his shoulders. "Oh well, so I'm not a historian," joked Vince.

"You are so silly. Go ahead and order the food," remarked Riya, bobbing her head back and forth as she spoke.

Vince chuckled then pulled his cell phone out of his coat pocket and began dialing.

Riya turned to Ovasta. "How about I go and bring Major inside then give him something to eat. You go ahead and get changed."

Ovasta shook her head in agreement and Riya left her on the sofa. Before coming all the way inside, Riya placed her shoes on the inside doormat, then headed into the kitchen to open a can of food for Major's dinner, something she'd done on many occasions. Ovasta went into her room and could hear Riya opening the door for Major and him running inside barking. He was happy to see her as always.

When Ovasta came into the dining room after having

changed into her pink silk pajamas and matching robe, Riya was seated. Vince had by then sat out glasses, soda, and paper plates and napkins on the oak dining room table. Ovasta sat down in one of the six chairs with a red floral pattern, rubbing her feet on the matching floral throw rug under the table. The red taffeta curtains against the cream-colored wallpaper provided the perfect accent for the room.

"Vee, I want all the details about the vote. Tell us what happened."

Vince let out a sigh. "Man oh man, women always want details. Isn't it enough that she won? Who cares what happened before that?"

Riya rolled her eyes at him. "I care. Could you please let her talk?"

"Sure. You ladies talk all you want. I'll wait for the food to come. Hopefully, it won't be much longer." Vince shook his head and went towards the living room.

Ovasta and Riya's giggles followed him as he left.

Riya threw her hand at him in a dismissive gesture. "Anyway tell me, Vee, how close was the vote?"

"At first, Phillip had received four votes and I hadn't received any. I can't tell you how upset I was about that. But then I received several in a row. All of a sudden, Phillip and I were tied up until the last vote. Everyone's eyes were on Mr. Gerard. You could cut the tension in the room with a knife. When he announced my name as having won, I could barely keep my composure. And of course, I already told you that Phillip hurried out after that. His friend, Samuel King, reluctantly shook my hand then he left as well."

"Well at least he had the decency to shake your hand. That Phillip is a sad character. He's too immature to be heading anything!"

Riya stopped talking upon hearing the doorbell ring. Vince answered the door and paid the delivery man for the food. "Alright, let's eat!" exclaimed Vince as he entered the room with a brown bag full of Chinese food in one hand and a bottle of champagne in the other.

"Hey, where'd you get the champagne?" asked Ovasta.

"I have a secret stash you don't know about," he chuckled.

"How can you have a secret stash at someone else's house?" questioned Riya, squinting with her lips pursed.

Vince laughed. "Don't get all worked up. It was in the back of the hall closet where I normally hang my coat. Besides, I don't hear my fiancée complaining."

"Okay, you two, knock it off so we can eat," ordered Ovasta, looking at both of them humorously.

"Thank you, honey," said Vince happily as he popped open the champagne, pouring a little into each glass. "I'd like to propose a toast to Miss Ovasta Kaiser —soon to be Mrs. Ovasta Parker — on her election as board president." All three raised their glasses toward each other and drank.

Riya hit her fork on the side of the glass creating a chiming noise. "I'd like to make a toast to the both of you on your engagement. I couldn't be happier. I love you both so much. . . I think it's time for a group hug." The trio hugged each other, filling the room with cheer. Riya looked at Vince slyly. "Vince, I need to ask you one question. What took you so long? You know Ovasta has been buying bridal magazines for the past four months."

"No, I didn't know," replied Vince, smiling.

"I'm not sure I believe you. Your eyes shifted to the left when you spoke. I read somewhere that means you're not being truthful," said Riya sarcastically.

"I took the Hippocratic Oath, I cannot tell a lie," he laughed.

"Oh, my God! We all know that oath doesn't apply to this situation!" exclaimed Riya while blinking her eyes swiftly several times in a row.

"Come on, let's go and look through some of the magazines. I already have a lot of ideas. Vince would you wash the dishes please?" asked Ovasta, as she gently interlocked her arm with Riya's tugging her away from Vince.

He blew her a kiss. "I sure will, sweetie."

Vince went into the kitchen and put a small amount of champagne in Major's water bowl. While he washed the dishes, Riya and Ovasta perused bridal magazines. Once it got late, Riya headed home. Vince stayed to watch the baseball game. Ovasta dozed on and off on the couch beside him while Major slept flat on his back, paws sprawled upward, head to one side, with his tongue dangling out of his mouth, on the floor near her feet.

TWO

Ralph Stacolli, Sr. drove his black BMW down the winding road to the gated community where he and his family lived. When he arrived at the gate, he was immediately waved in by two members of the family's security team. He took the driveway to the right towards his father's house. His father, Joseph "the Boss" Stacolli, had recently been released from the hospital following a bout with pneumonia. Ralph was CFO for several car dealerships owned and operated by the Stacolli family. Many community members and law officials suspected criminal activity was behind the dealership's success. However, no member of the family had ever been convicted of any major offense.

Ralph rang the doorbell and was greeted by Maria, the family's most trusted housekeeper. Maria was in her early sixties and had been with the family for over thirty years. She moved her stout body aside, opening the door a little further to let Ralph in the house. His six-foot-three, nearly four-hundred-pound frame filled the entrance. His mother, Stella Stacolli, met him in the vestibule. Ralph tilted his body close to his much shorter mother allowing her to salute him on both cheeks. Still spry at almost 75 years old, she had very few wrinkles in her face. Her short, cropped, silvery-gray hair glistened like fresh snow on Mount Everest. Clad mostly in dresses, Ralph believed his mother was the epitome of womanhood.

"Your father was wondering when you were coming to see him."

Ralph held his head down shamefully. "Yeah, I know. I should have come over yesterday when you told me he was home. Where is he?"

"Where he always is, sitting in his favorite chair in the den. Go ahead in there and sit with him for a while. I'm going to the kitchen to fix your father something to eat. Would you like something, too?"

Ralph smiled broadly. "Sure thing, Ma!"

"Of course you would," she giggled while pinching his left cheek.

Ralph turned away and entered the den. His father was stretched out comfortably in his favorite dark-brown recliner chair right in front of the big-screen television. To some degree, his father reminded him of Santa Claus minus the long beard— the white hair which was all but absent from the crown of his head, sparkling blue eyes, chubby cheeks, small circular nose and a round belly.

"Hey, Boss, how are you doing?" asked Ralph. He'd called his father "Boss" ever since he could remember, like all the other kids in the neighborhood where he and his three brothers grew up.

"I'm doing a lot better than I was last week. Come and

give your father a hug." Boss extended his arms towards Ralph with a small gap-toothed smile on his face. Ralph leaned over to hug his father who was now sitting up.

"Sorry I didn't visit you much while you were in the hospital, but I thought about you every minute. I couldn't stand to see you that way," mumbled Ralph, avoiding eye contact with his father.

"Don't worry about it, son, you're here now and that's all that matters. I did see a lot of Junnie though." Junnie was Ralph's 16-year-old son, Ralph Stacolli, Jr. "He's a good boy. So helpful to me in the hospital. I liked having him around. He gave your mother a much-needed break. You would've thought she was the on-call nurse the way she was acting while I was there." Boss' laughter turned into a dry hacking cough.

Patrick, Ralph's youngest brother, came into the den. Ralph always joked Patrick was his twin. Same height, eye and hair color, with two exceptions—12 years younger and one hundred and twenty pounds lighter. Patrick hugged his father and Ralph, then sat down on the brown velour couch.

"So, what are the two of you talking about?" asked Patrick.

"I was telling him about how Junnie took care of me during my stay in the hospital," explained Joseph.

Patrick made a faint sighing noise and cut his eyes slightly to the right at the mention of Junnie's name. Noticing, Ralph leaned close to Patrick and glared scornfully.

"Listen, Patrick, he is your nephew and my son. If you have a problem with him, bring it to me and we can handle it man to man," Ralph's voice began to elevate as he spoke to his brother.

"Ralph, I didn't say a word, so why are you getting so upset?"

Ralph's greenish-brown eyes pierced Patrick's. "You're right! You didn't *say* anything but I saw the expression on your face and I heard you sigh. Are you trying to tell me I'm stupid? I know what your problem is. You're upset because my son does not want to carry on the family business. Well, for the record, it's his choice. He wants to go to college and become a lawyer. You know we need some attorneys from time to time. Wouldn't it be better to be represented by family? Someone we can actually trust."

"Yes, Ralph, you are absolutely right."

Hearing the commotion, Stella rushed into the den. "Are the two of you arguing again? What are you talking about?"

Ralph rolled his eyes towards his mother. "We were talking about Junnie. It would seem that Patrick has a problem with him because every time anyone mentions my son's name, Patrick either smirks or makes some type of negative facial expression. I don't like it. I don't like it at all."

Stella eyed both of her sons in disgust. "I remember the last time the two of you had a discussion about Junnie. It ended with Patrick's face being slammed into the dining room table. He spent the night in the emergency room with a broken nose and multiple face lacerations." Her voice got louder as she spoke.

"Ma, I apologized for the incident. I paid for Patrick's

medical expenses and promised to never hit him again. I always keep my promises. Always," replied Ralph almost pleading with his mother to prove a point.

Stella put her hand on her left hip while wagging her right index finger at her sons. "Listen, I remember what you said and did. But right now things seem to be headed in that same direction. I could hear you two talking from the kitchen and it didn't sound friendly at all. I want the both of you to stop acting like children. Your father is recuperating and does not need this type of stress. If anything else like that ever happens again, I'm telling you both that you'll regret it. I won't tolerate this behavior another minute." Stella looked at Boss who was still seated across the room. His grimace suggested he wanted this conversation over as soon as possible. She sauntered over to him and rubbed his shoulders. Boss always enjoyed her massages and she wanted him to return to a more relaxed state. "We're family. I want us to show each other love and stop all the bickering and fighting." Stella paused for a moment. Afterward, she let out a long breath then continued. Her tone drastically lighter. "How about I cook all of us a nice dinner tonight? Come on, call your wives and children. I want everybody to come over. Let's eat dinner together. Now I want my boys to play nice and hug each other."

Ralph and Patrick gave each other a stiff embrace. Their mother ambled over to both of them, pinching each of their cheeks. "Aww, now that's what I like to see." Neither of them spoke. Neither dared sass their mother. "I want you both to go home, wash up, and bring my daughters and grandbabies back with you."

Stella headed back into the kitchen while Ralph and Patrick said their goodbyes to Joseph but left the house without acknowledging each other. All four of Joseph's sons and their families lived within the same gated community as their parents. The surrounding stone walls and glass-enclosed guard entrance made it appear more like a military compound. Due to the enormousness of the houses, it took almost ten minutes to drive from one house to the next. On the way home, Patrick shuddered at the thought of having to deal with Ralph again today. He loved Ralph but knew he was in denial about Junnie. Patrick also resented his father showing Junnie favoritism over the other grandchildren. Always bragging on how smart he was . . . giving him money . . . taking him and his friends on lavish trips overseas. Patrick did not want to go to his parents' house for dinner today and wished he could figure out how to get out of it.

The whole Stacolli clan gathered for dinner by 6:00 p.m. Stella was adamant about starting dinner promptly at 6:15 p.m. Normally, they ate dinner together on Sundays. However, due to Boss' recent hospitalization, dinner had been postponed for the past two weeks. Boss and Stella were eager to have the family gather as soon as possible. For them, family time was more important than anything else.

Stella had hired help but would not allow anyone else to cook dinner for family gatherings. She prided herself in being able to cook large, delicious meals. Sometimes her daughters-in-law would help if she were under the weather. Whether sick or well, Stella was the boss in the kitchen. Today's menu consisted of raspberry vinaigrette salad, orechiette with sausage and beans, and roasted vegetables. The adults usually drank Prosecco, the children a special punch created by Junnie.

The family ate in the oversized dining room which Stella dedicated to eating and entertaining. The simple paisley pattern on the wooden upholstered chairs, family portraits on the pale blue walls, and wooden hutch in the corner of the room helped create a homey environment. Boss sat at one end of the table which was covered in a vintage-lace tablecloth crocheted by his late mother-in-law. Stella usually sat on his right side. Normally, Ralph would sit at the left side of his father, next to his wife, Cynthia, and Junnie.

Once everyone was seated, Boss cleared his throat to gain their attention. "I'd like Junnie to sit in his father's place next to me at the dinner table," he demanded. Ralph appeared puzzled as he got up to trade places with his son who appeared confused as well. Junnie began to sweat profusely. His green eyes were wide with alarm as he awkwardly moved his tall frame around his father in order to switch seats. Once seated, he patted his forehead with a napkin from off the table. For a brief moment, there was silence. Boss observed the facial expressions of everyone at the table, particularly those of his sons John, Carl, and Patrick. "Does anyone have a problem with my request?" He leaned closer to the table, leering.

Patrick spoke up. "Boss, no one has a problem with it. We're simply wondering what's going on. This is the first time that I can ever remember the seating arrangement being changed with the exception of having a guest. It's kind of odd, that's all. We thought maybe you were trying to tell us something."

Boss rolled his eyes and shook his head from side to side, eventually sighing. "Can't a man have his eldest grandson sit with him at dinner without there being a motive?"

Patrick shrugged his shoulders and forced a smile on his face. "Sure, Boss. Your house, your rules."

Patrick made a sharp, quick glance at John and Carl, which they were careful not to acknowledge. All parties, even the children, stared into their plates. In an instance, the chatter was replaced by the gulping of food and the high-pitched sound of forks scratching across fine china. No one wanted to be accused of disrespecting the Boss, not even with a look. He didn't respond well to any perceived insolence.

In an apparent effort to change the mood, Stella lifted her glass towards Joseph. "I'd like to propose a toast to family. No matter what happens, we have to stick together." Everyone raised their glasses. "To family."

Stacolli family tradition was to exchange hugs prior to going home. Patrick made his way around the room, his father's eyes following him. He knew his father wanted to ensure he not only hugged Junnie but Ralph as well. Although he felt a little uneasy, he managed to maintain a cool exterior. Gently, he put his arm around Ralph's neck. Next, he hugged Junnie under Ralph's watchful eye.

"Love you, Uncle Pat," whispered Junnie as they embraced.

"I love you, too." Patrick noticed his father watching with a smile from across the room. He was relieved to have his father's approval.

Patrick turned towards his children who were standing near their grandmother and waved his hand towards the door. "Come on, kids. Let's go. You know you have to get ready for school tomorrow," said Patrick while nearing the door.

Michelle, Patrick's wife, joined her family as they walked out the door. The children ran ahead of them towards the house.

"You rushed out of the house faster than I've ever seen. Is everything okay?" questioned Michelle as she grabbed her husband's hand.

"I was really ready to go. I feel like Boss is positioning Junnie to play a bigger role in the family business. Did you see how he was watching me like a hawk while I hugged Junnie? What is that about?"

"Oh, honey, I don't think you should get all worked up about it. Whatever you get from Boss, even if it's not what you believe you deserve, it will all work out in the end. You know, you're the smartest of all your father's sons. Smart enough to double your earnings." Michelle puckered her lips and Patrick gave her a quick peck.

"Thanks, sweetie. I can always count on you for support. You know I have a problem with that kid."

"I know. I know. But Junnie's got a good heart. And remember he is still a child. You never know what he'll grow up to be."

"Well, he's certainly more even-tempered than his father. He definitely got that from his mother." Patrick sniggered. "However, I do think that I want to discuss some things with my brothers."

Michelle shook her head. "I'm not sure what you'll be discussing, but please be civil won't you?"

"Have you ever known me to be anything else?"

Michelle smirked. "We both know I shouldn't answer that."

Patrick let out hearty laughter.

"You know you sound like a mad scientist, right?" questioned Michelle joining in the laughter.

"Get in the house woman. The kids are already inside," commanded Patrick lightheartedly as he opened the door.

Only moments after arriving home, Patrick called Carl. "Can you get with John? I'd like to meet for lunch tomorrow at our favorite spot?"

"Sure, I can. We definitely have to discuss what went on tonight. I know John will want to talk about it as well. Do you want me to call *him*?" Patrick knew Carl was not talking about John or Ralph.

"Most definitely. If he really wants to be a part of this family then he needs to take part in what's going on."

"I'll see what his availability is and get back with you later."

"Tell him he needs to be there. We've got to make a plan. Things seem to be going awry. We need to set them straight. I think it all stems from the conversation I had with Boss, Ralph, and Ma earlier today. When I went to see Boss today, he and Ralph were talking about Junnie. Sometimes I can't help but cringe when Boss mentions Junnie's name. You already know what I don't like about him. Although Boss tried to make everyone believe that moving Junnie next to him had no meaning. We all know better. Everything Boss does is calculated. I believe he may be considering letting Junnie be a major part in the business or giving him a little more of the inheritance than he deserves. Michelle says I shouldn't worry about it. I love her but this is my future we're talking about. Actually, it's all of our futures."

"Exactly. That's why we should all be involved. I'll make a phone call and definitely stress to him that he needs to be there. Good night, Pat, see you tomorrow."

Patrick hung up the phone and headed towards the bathroom to take a long hot shower.

THREE

I t was one month before the inaugural ball where Ovasta would officially be installed as the next president of the board of directors. She and Riya decided to not only go shopping for dinner dresses but for Ovasta's wedding dress as well.

Riya drove to Ovasta's house and left her car in the driveway. Together, they drove about thirty minutes to the west side shopping outlet stores.

"Why don't we go straight to a bridal shop before we do anything else?" asked Riya as they were exiting the highway.

"That sounds great! Isn't it wonderful we no longer have to window shop like we had to do as undergraduates?"

Both smiled as they recalled how scarce food was during their college years. Somehow, one of them would find a meal which they'd share. Those hard times created an inseparable bond between them.

Ovasta pulled into the shopping lot closest to several of her favorite stores.

"Riya, let's go into the Designer Dress Boutique. I believe they have some Vera Wang dresses."

Riya beamed. "That's right, my friend, spare no expense. You'll be the most beautiful bride ever. While we're there, let's look at bridesmaids' dresses, too. Of course, mine will be a little different and prettier than the other two dresses. Seeing as how I'm the maid-of-honor and all."

Ovasta ignored her friend's comment. "I'm glad Vince's cousin, Sandra, and my cousin, Gwen, wanted to be a part of the wedding party. They're both really good people. I can't wait to see Sandra again. Since she got married last year and moved to Los Angeles, we haven't seen much of her. It will be good to reconnect."

"You're right. I've always liked them both. You and Vince have great families. Well, here we are!" exclaimed Riya happily as they entered the store.

"Alright, let's get this party started."

Happy to be together, they spent several hours shopping at different boutiques. Both Ovasta and Riya purchased dresses for the Director's Ball along with several other items. The excursion ended with the pair getting something to eat at a nearby bar and grill.

"I think we got some great bargains today, don't you, Vee? I'm glad we decided to look in other stores before buying wedding dresses though," stated Riya as they were seated at the restaurant table by the server.

Ovasta didn't reply. She was peering out of the window towards the south side of the street even as they were walking towards their table.

"Vee, did you hear me? What are you looking at?" Riya's high-pitched voice finally caught Ovasta's attention.

"Phillip. Sometimes I think he's following me."

"You mean Phillip Michaels? What would he be doing on this side of town?"

"I don't know but that was certainly him and I don't trust him. I've always had a sense that he was hiding something."

Ovasta stopped talking when she saw the waitress coming towards them with two menus in her hand.

"Hello, ladies. My name is Sara. I'll be your waitress today. Can I get you something to drink?" she queried while placing a menu in front of each of them.

"Actually, we don't need the menu. We'll both have a sprite, a large order of honey mustard wings, and some potato skins," said Riya

"Also, can you bring two plates? We're going to split the entrees. I have to say, you guys have the best wings ever," stated Ovasta.

"Thank you so much! I'll get those drinks right out for you." The waitress picked up the menus and walked away.

"Okay. Where were we?" asked Ovasta while watching the waitress leave.

Riya thought back. "I agree with what you said. Phillip is definitely hiding something. You remember how he got married three years ago and then got divorced eight months later. Who does that? You know it had to be something wrong. Maybe his ex-wife discovered what the issue was and couldn't deal with it. You never really know."

"Right. Then shortly after the divorce she up and left town. It was so all of a sudden. Since then, he's become very withdrawn and never talks about his life outside of work. Even when he smiles, there is sadness in his eyes."

"I know. But you can't worry about it. He's never really liked you because you've always beat him at everything. He's a jealous-hearted narcissistic person." Riya paused. She gazed out of the window in an effort to see if she could see Phillip outside. "Remember, even before you both started at the hospital, he wanted to be the chairman of the board of directors for the National Adoptions Agency. Instead, you were picked. Before that, *you* were chosen to be their national spokesperson although Phillip practically begged for the position."

The waitress brought the drinks and two straws, setting them on the table, along with two empty plates.

Ovasta pulled the paper off the straw, placed it into her glass and took a sip. "I remember. I was the face of the agency for four years. I received so many invitations to speak on the agency's behalf that I asked Phillip to fill in for me."

Ovasta recalled Phillip being upset about her appointment but remembered him being quite pleased to represent her on many occasions. She thought they had become pretty close during those years. Phillip was adopted when he was about two years old. He didn't know his father. After he was born, his mother's post-partum depression was so severe she ceased to take care of him. Eventually, he was unable to thrive. At that point, Child Protective Services removed him from the home. Not long after his mother was deemed by the courts well enough to care for him, she was killed in a car accident. Consequently, he was adopted by Mr. and Mrs. Samuel Michaels. The Michaels family had been good friends with his mother and her family for years. They had no problem caring for him.

Like Phillip, Ovasta was adopted by her maternal grandparents after her parents, died in a car crash. While in high school, she volunteered at the National Adoptions Agency. Phillip was already a volunteer there and the two became very good friends. Each spoke to children about the heartaches they had encountered by not growing up with their biological parents or not having a sense of belonging. Additionally, they attended adoption mixers where prospective adoptive parents came to meet children in foster care.

During the year following high school graduation, Ovasta helped Phillip care for his ailing parents with whom she had become very close. When Mrs. Michaels was diagnosed with colon cancer, Ovasta drove her to the hospital on a weekly basis for chemotherapy. Phillip stayed home with Mr. Michaels who had triple bypass surgery around the same time Mrs. Michaels started chemo. Mrs. Michaels died during Phillip's freshman year of college. Mr. Michaels passed away six months later.

Days after the passing of Mr. Michaels, Phillip confided in her that a man showed up at his home claiming to be his biological father. Phillip appeared extremely distraught by the meeting and was literally shaking as he spoke to her about it. He explained how his father met his mother at a restaurant where she was a waitress. His dad started out dining there because of the great food but began frequenting the place in order to see her. Falling for her quick wit, lovely smile, and beautifully framed build. Although she knew he was married, they began dating. He lavished her with clothing, jewelry, money, and even a brand new car.

Phillip said the relationship ended abruptly because his mother insisted that his father leave his wife — something he had no intention of doing. Subsequently, the affair ended and his dad stopped dining at the restaurant where his mother worked.

After roughly four months had passed, a family member informed his dad they had seen her and she was pregnant. Phillip was assured his dad didn't know of the pregnancy prior to breaking off the relationship. He told Phillip he always sent her money to take care of him and even attended her funeral. His dad also knew Mr. and Mrs. Michaels and helped them financially but couldn't be more a part of Phillip's life because of his wife. When Phillip became an adult, his dad's wife was more accepting of him. He invited Phillip to come and meet his siblings and be a part of their family.

After meeting his father, Phillip began to change. It appeared he was always competing against her. During their college years, he attempted to find out what her GPA was in an effort to discover whose was higher. After she was chosen by their cohorts to make the commencement speech, Phillip literally stopped speaking to her. She had long decided not to accept blame for being chosen over him for several positions throughout their careers.

Ovasta wished she and Phillip could have remained close as he'd become like a brother to her. They had even decided to go to the same college together for moral support.

"Riya, do you realize I've supported Phillip and his late parents?"

"I know you have. Don't worry about it. You did the right thing by helping them and it came from your heart. If for some reason Phillip has decided to no longer be friends with you—even acting as if you're his archenemy—there is nothing you can do about it but move on."

Ovasta sighed and could feel the blood rushing towards her face. "That's exactly what Vince said. And it's definitely something I've tried to do. For the record, it really hurt how abruptly things ended. He simply changed overnight and I have no idea why. However, I can't afford to let anything hold me back."

"I know it hurts. Things like that always do. But, you've always been a driven, career-oriented woman. Once I see you set your mind to do something, I consider it done."

"You're pretty goal-oriented yourself. That's probably why we get along so well."

The waitress brought the food and placed it in the middle of the table. "I hope you enjoy it, ladies."

"Thanks," responded Riya as she put hand sanitizer in her palm. "It sounds like Phillip's biological father isn't as great of an influence on him as Mr. Michael's was."

Ovasta used some sanitizer as well then put a potato skin and several wings on her plate. She shrugged in response to Riya's comment. "I don't know. I've never met the man. I think Phillip had too many life changes in a short span of time. Losing both parents and then meeting your real father all within a year is a lot, but it doesn't excuse his behavior."

Riya picked up a wing. "You're right. I guess it's not our job to psychoanalyze him. Let's enjoy our food. The meal is on me since you spent so much money on your dinner dress."

"Thanks, Riya. I appreciate it."

"No problem. I'll probably need to borrow it back sometime in the near future." Riya looked at Ovasta with peering eyes and pouted lips. "For the record, it *was* Phillip. I saw him, too, shortly after you mentioned it. But I don't believe he was following us. He didn't even see us sitting here. You're getting a little paranoid in your old age."

"What do you mean in my old age? I am only one month older than you are."

"Well, you are one month closer to receiving Social Security than I am."

They both snickered and for the next half hour, discussed wedding plans prior to heading home.

FOUR

As Patrick drove home after having had lunch with his brothers, he began to reconsider whether or not the plan they discussed was really necessary. There was already enough bad blood between family members ever since Boss gave Ralph control over a larger share of the family business. Upon Boss' death, Ralph was due to inherit four times what the rest of would receive. Even with that in mind, Patrick thought he and his brothers were going too far. Moreover, if their plan was ever discovered by their father or Ralph, God only knows what would happen. Perspiration formed on Patrick's forehead and underarms. He rolled up his car windows and turned on the air conditioner. He decided to speak to his brothers in an effort to change their minds. It was finally time to bury the hatchet.

After being waved through the gate by security, Patrick took a right turn in his car and headed home prior to going to his parents' house for dinner. His wife saw him as he entered the house. "You are perspiring heavily, please tell me why my cool, confident husband is so upset?" inquired

Michelle as she put her hands on his face, their warmth like the sun on the morning dew.

"I had a lunch meeting with some of my brothers today and I believe this feud with Ralph is getting seriously out of hand. We came up with a plan that I don't believe is in the best interest of our family. I thought about it all the way home. There is no way we should be doing what we were talking about. It is horrendous to say the least. I hope my brothers will understand why I've decided changed our plans." He embraced Michelle. The faint odor of jasmine in her perfume calmed his nerves. "I would like to go to my parents' house today and make amends with Ralph and Junnie. What we were planning won't solve a thing and will do more harm than good," he stated, resting his head on her shoulder and running his hands through her waist-length black hair.

"I believe you can do whatever you set your mind to do," she replied sweetly. Patrick lifted his head off her shoulder, caressing her gently.

"I'm going upstairs to take a shower. I'm looking forward to a peaceful dinner with my family."

After changing clothes, Patrick, Michelle, and their two tweens, decided to walk to Boss and Stella's house. As soon as they exited their home, the kids hurriedly ran ahead of them towards the winding pathway to their grandparents' home.

"Be sure to stay on the sidewalk, kids. You know how fast your uncle Carl tends to drive through here," cautioned Michelle as they rushed past her.

"We will," they replied in unison.

Patrick laughed. "I'm so glad they get along."

"Like two peas in a pod." Michelle glanced forward, her eyes dancing with joy at her children.

Patrick lamented. "I wish the same could be said about my relationship with Ralph. You know, I was thinking about suggesting to the family that we have a party for Dad's seventieth birthday. Maybe use it as a means of making peace. It could be the start of a new chapter in all of our lives. I'm so sick of all the bickering and bad blood between us."

Michelle gazed lovingly into his eyes. "Sweetie, I'm so proud of you. I know this decision didn't come easily. But your idea is great. I'm sure your mother would be pleased."

Patrick glanced at his wife smiling as the two ambled slowly to his parents' home, holding hands. They enjoyed the outdoors. Family vacations were spent windsurfing at Carolina Beach and fishing at the Lake of the Ozarks in Missouri. Some winters were spent in the Alps for skiing. Michelle always joked Patrick skied so well he should have been on the U.S. Olympic team. As they moseyed along, Patrick decided to increase his pace the moment he saw in the distance his children had already entered their grandparents' home. Ralph stepped out of the door, beckoning them to come in. Patrick waved at his brother. He was genuinely glad to see him.

Upon entering their parents' home, Patrick wrapped his arms around Ralph's shoulders. Ralph pulled slightly away from him, as he was not expecting such a cheerful greeting.

Ralph observed his brother and beamed. "Thank you

for the heartfelt embrace. I appreciate it. Now come on in. Everyone else has been here for at least a half an hour. I'm going in the back for a few minutes and watch the kids." He patted his youngest brother on the back and moved away from the doorway, letting Michelle into the house after hugging her.

Patrick extended his open hand behind him which Michelle grabbed without hesitation.

They were greeted by Stella when they walked in. "What took you so long? Your kids have been here for ten minutes already."

Patrick kissed his mother on the cheek. "We took the scenic route," he chuckled.

Stella smirked, sloping her eyes upward at her son. "Ha, ha, ha. Dinner isn't quite ready yet. Pat, why don't you go in the den with your father? Michelle and I will go into the kitchen in order to finish things up."

Patrick nodded his head in agreement. It always pleased him that other than the hired help, Michelle was one of the few people his mother invited into the kitchen. He always felt his wife was a better cook than his mother but would never admit it to anyone. Not even Michelle.

When Patrick entered the den, John and Carl were already there. Both favored their father in his younger years. "Hey, fellas, I didn't know you were here already," he jested.

"Really. Yes, you did! 'Cuz you're always the last one to arrive," mocked Carl. His plump lips twisted to one side.

Patrick strolled over to his father in order to hug him.

He did not always agree with his dad, but truly loved him. "Boss, how has your week been so far?"

"I can't complain. What good would it do anyway?"

Patrick sniggered at his father's response. He deliberately sat down on the couch, squeezing between Carl and John. Ralph entered the den, standing next to his father. He had been outside on the patio watching his nieces and nephews run around the backyard. Patrick, Carl, and John watched as Ralph embraced their father. Patrick cleared his throat in an effort to get everyone's attention.

"I would like to propose that we have a birthday party for Boss. I can't remember the last time we had a celebration of any kind."

Boss raised one eyebrow. "You better ask your mother what she thinks. My birthday is only three weeks away. You know how she hates last-minute plans."

Stella appeared in the doorway of the den, wiping her hands on her apron. "What last-minute plans are you boys talking about?"

"Hey, Ma, I'd like to have a birthday party for Dad," Patrick explained.

Stella put her hand on her right hip. "I think that's a great idea but why did you wait so late to start discussing it?"

"Sorry about that, Ma, but I already know a great location. I'm sure all of your daughters-in-law will pitch in. Anyway, I will pay for a caterer so you won't have to cook a thing."

Stella squinted her eyes, glaring at Patrick. "I'm very

happy you want to do this, but this is the most you've ever offered to help. Is there anything going on *we* should know about?"

Stella always used the royal "we". Everyone knew she was only talking about herself and Boss.

Patrick leaned forward. "The truth is, John, Carl, and I went to lunch and had a discussion about the party." Patrick glanced at each of them. Mouths agape. Faces partially flushed. Neither could believe Patrick was going to tell their parents—or Ralph—about the secret meeting and their plans. Patrick gave them a comforting smile that did not seem to relieve their apprehension. "At lunch, we discussed how much we wanted to bury the hatchet. A decision was made to end the discord between us. After all, we are family." Patrick glanced up at Ralph with a lump in his throat. "Ralph, we've had our differences in the past. But I do believe with some effort we can move past them. I'll try if you will."

Ralph shook his head in agreement but remained quiet.

Patrick turned to his parents. "Dad, let's make this party a celebration of new beginnings. The three of us want the latter part of your life to be filled with love and laughter. Lately, all we've had is arguing, bickering." Patrick paused, surveying the room. "I'm very sorry for any heartache that I have ever caused any of my family," he continued.

"I love you, son." Boss' rough voice began to crack.

Stella waltzed across the room, saluting her three sons on their cheeks. "I have never been prouder of you than I am today."

Joseph got up from his recliner. All his sons rose as they saw their father rising to his feet. Apologies were made among the brothers for past aggressive behaviors towards each other. When they were finished, Michelle entered the room to announce dinner was ready.

The family entered the dining room, taking their usual places. Visibly absent from the table was Junnie.

Ralph saw Boss eye the empty chair were Junnie normally sat and apologized for Junnie's tardiness. "Boss, in case you were wondering. Your grandson is at the library studying with some friends for a chemistry test. He should be here in the next half hour."

Boss nodded his head. "Don't worry about it, son, school is important. I know he'd be here if he could."

Stella interrupted the conversation by hitting her fork on the side of her glass producing a chiming noise. "I'd like to give kudos to John, Carl, and Pat for volunteering to throw their father a birthday party. It is only three weeks away so we have a lot of work to do."

Michelle winked at Patrick, placing her hand under the table and rubbing his thigh.

Stella raised her glass, as she did at every family gathering. The rest of the family members followed suit. "To family."

Ralph's phone rang while he was eating. "Hello, son. Are you on your way?" questioned

Ralph vociferously. After pausing for a moment and listening, he turned to his father. "Junnie said he's at the door.

He wants to know if his friend from school could come in to meet the family and eat dinner."

Patrick watched as Boss smiled then motioned for Ralph to get the door. He noticed Ralph hesitate then scan the room observing the rest of the family. When Ralph eyed him, Patrick was sure Ralph could see disdain radiating from his countenance. Normally, dinner was reserved for only family. Even he never had anyone over for dinner. Once more and again it seemed Junnie could do no wrong in the eyes of his parents. However, for the sake of peace, he decided not to say anything.

After looking around, Ralph spoke loudly into his phone. "Sure, son. I believe everyone here would love to meet your friend."

From the tone in Ralph's voice, Patrick almost knew he was being mocked. He watched angrily as Ralph excused himself, pushed away from the table, and moved leisurely out of the dining room.

While he was gone, Boss asked Maria, the housekeeper, to make another place setting for Junnie's friend. Within a few minutes, Ralph, Junnie, and his classmate entered the dining room. Smirking, Patrick examined Charles's short but athletic build, freckles and red hair and noticed how Junnie grabbed Ralph. Holding on to Ralph's midsection for dear life. Like he was afraid of being swept away by some great and mighty wind.

Stella rose from her chair when they came in. "How's my oldest grandson doing?" she asked as she kissed him on the cheek.

Junnie let go of his father in order to hug her. "I'm fine, Grandma." Junnie looked around and addressed his family. "First off, I'd like to thank everyone for being okay with me being both late and bringing a guest with no advance notice. Secondly, I want everyone to meet my friend Charles Jones. He has been helping me study and probably has the highest GPA in the whole school!"

Everyone's not alright with it. We didn't have a choice, thought Patrick holding his head down. When he looked up, Boss was staring at him. Almost like he knew what Patrick was thinking. On most occasions, his father's face said a lot without saying anything. At times it was down right out scary. Although Patrick never felt as if his father would physically harm him, he still didn't want to get on his bad side. At this moment, all Patrick wanted to do is eat as fast as possible so that he and his family could go home.

"Charles, you don't mind if I give you a hug, do you?" asked Stella happily.

"No, ma'am."

Stella hugged Charles then pinched him on the cheek. "Any friend of my grandson is more than welcome in my home."

Charles smiled revealing beautiful white teeth. "Thank you for the invitation."

"Welcome." Boss moved his right hand in a downwards motion. "Now sit down and eat. The food is getting cold. Maria has already prepared a plate for both of you."

Charles sat down and started eating immediately.

"So, Charles, what is your favorite subject?" inquired Stella.

Charles answered upon finishing a forkful of food he had recently placed in his mouth. "I love math. I want to teach it one day."

"Is that what the two of you have been studying?"

"No, ma'am. We've actually been working on Physics."

"Physics. I thought that was only for high school seniors. Wow, you're both handsome and smart," gushed Stella.

"He's also very athletic and is on the football team," interjected Junnie.

"Yes, I love sports as well," added Charles while stuffing more food into his mouth.

"I hope you are enjoying dinner, young man?" Stella appeared amused by the pace at which Charles gobbled his food.

"The food is delicious, ma'am. Thank you for having me over for dinner." Charles gulped down some punch out of his glass after responding.

"No problem, you are always welcome in my home. I do hope to see you again sometime soon." Stella's eyes broadened with glee as she addressed Junnie. "I wanted to mention to you that we have decided to have a birthday party for your grandfather?"

Junnie poked out his lips as his glower went around the room. "Really, nobody told me about any party."

"Now, now. There's no need to be upset. We didn't have

time to tell you. Your uncles just announced the idea today. We have a lot of planning to do."

"Grandma, you know I'll help in any way I can!" Junnie turned and looked at Charles. "Hopefully, you can help. Maybe you could come and help run some errands for us if you're not too busy that day."

"I'm sure I could clear my schedule," replied Charles smiling at Junnie.

Junnie grinned. He put his hand on top of Charles' and rubbed it lightly in a circular motion.

Patrick's jaw dropped. "I knew it!" He pounded his fist down, sending shock waves across the dining room table.

"You knew what?" replied Ralph as he swiftly pushed his chair back from the table.

Patrick ignored Ralph and spoke to his father. "Did you see what they did, Boss? Junnie and his friend are disrespecting your home."

"B-b-but . . . we didn't do anything," stuttered Junnie. Tears tumbled down his now flushed cheeks.

"How about we excuse the children from the table, then we can have this discussion. Maria, would you watch the children as they play outdoors?" Boss's voice was eerily calm.

"Yes, sir." Maria pointed towards the glass door which led to the backyard. Hastily, the children got up from the table and went outdoors. As he was leaving, Junnie glanced back at Patrick who was peering back at him. Patrick's eyes grew smaller the longer he stared at his nephew, piercing Junnie's soul.

His glare cut short by Boss' voice. "Patrick, must I remind you that certain conversations should never be held in front of the children?"

"Forgive me, Boss, for not waiting. I became furious when I saw Junnie outing himself in your home. Please, look outside and tell me what you see?"

Through the glass door, Charles could be seen holding Junnie in his arms while Junnie weeping incessantly.

"You know what I see? I see a boy who is embarrassed by his uncle's rude behavior," replied Boss very firmly.

Patrick heard Ralph grumble and turned towards him. Borrowed lines formed on Patrick's forehead. "Why are you always grumbling, Ralph? Try using your words. Say what's on your mind. If you can explain to us what you see outside then go ahead. I'd love to hear it."

Ralph's brows lowered over his squinted eyes. "I don't appreciate your mocking tone! This kind of stuff right here is why we don't get along. You're always trying to bait me. Then everyone gets upset when I lash out at you in anger."

Michelle spoke up, her voice cracking, "Is that what you call it? Lashing out. You've done more than lash out. Remember, you broke my husband's nose."

"Yeah, Ralph, that wasn't right. We have enough enemies without fighting one another," added Carl while wagging his finger at his brother.

"As I said to Ma earlier today, I apologized for that and it won't happen again. Can we please change the subject?"

"He's trying guys. Why don't you cut him some slack?" questioned Ralph's wife while rubbing his back.

An angry silence blanketed the room as everyone resumed eating.

Moments later, Patrick dropped his fork on the plate and spoke up. His tone deadpan and without reservation. "Ralph, you still haven't answered the question. What did you think was going on outside between your son and that Charles boy?"

"Absolutely nothing!" shouted Ralph while pounding his right hand on the table. "I can't believe you restarted this conversation when it was clearly over. For the record, we all know my son took a vow of chastity. He's not involved with anyone. Male or female!"

"Heh. Some vow. You know what your problem is, Ralph? You don't want to admit the truth. Your son is gay!"

Ralph sprang up, lunging to Patrick's side of the table with arms extended. Shaking the table and knocking over several drinks.

Patrick swiftly slid his chair backwards in order to escape his brother's grip and stood up. Both John and Carl swiftly stood up beside him. Breathing heavily, nostrils flared, narrowed eyes. Like raging bulls preparing to stampede the matador. Ralph's wife pulled at the back of his shirt screaming at him in an attempt to get him to sit down.

Stella pulled her red carbon fiber finished Glock 17, which had her initials engraved on the side of the barrel, from the holster which was secured to the underside of the table. *Bang . . . Bang . . . Bang!* She lifted the gun straight up in the air and shot several holes in the dining room ceiling, barely missing the glass chandelier. All parties froze. For a moment, time stood still. "I never met a target I couldn't shoot. Now, boys, I want you to sit down," she yelled, waving the gun back and forth from one side of the table with Patrick, Carl, and John to the other side with where Ralph was. Each sat down in his chair. Stella put the gun on the table beside her. Breathing heavily, she wiped the ceiling plaster out of her hair and from the table in front of her.

Boss swept plaster from his head then regarded his wife's eyes as he slid the gun away from her. "You boys have upset my wife. I take umbrage to that. It's probably best if you leave right now. Be sure to apologize to her on your way out. We'll discuss this later when everyone cools down. And, of course, the four of you will split the cost of repairing the celling. I want it done within the next two days." Boss began to suck his teeth. It was a sure sign he was very angry. He turned and waved to Maria to bring the children inside the house as she had been watching the whole ordeal through the glass ever since the shots were fired.

Quickly, she ushered the children in. Their parents rose from the table, approaching Stella with caution. One after another, they kissed her on the cheek, apologizing for being disrespectful to her home.

"We are still having a birthday party for my husband as we planned. I'll contact each of you later to formalize the details." Stella inspected the faces of all parties in the room. Her stares crawled all over them. Each head bowed in agreement upon leaving the room.

Junnie and Charles were the last of the children to come into the house from the backyard.

Boss spread out his arms in the boys' direction, giving both a big hug. "I'm sorry about tonight. Please forgive my family and know this will never happen again. I hope you'll come back because we'd love to have you."

"Thank you, sir, I'd be glad to come again." Charles and Junnie left the dining room and went to the foyer where Ralph was waiting for them.

"I'll drive you home, Charles. Call your parents and let them know you're on your way," said Ralph.

Patrick was standing in the foyer as well leering at Ralph, Charles, and Junnie. He stepped outside after they left and spoke to John and Carl who were waiting on him. "I tried to make peace with Ralph but to no avail. We're sticking to our original plan. Let's have lunch tomorrow in order to finalize things." All three saw Ralph leave without acknowledging him. It was the first time they ever ended dinner without a hug.

FIVE

With a lot of hard work and collaboration, the day of Boss's seventieth birthday had finally arrived. Stella and Boss were at home getting dressed. Boss stood in the bedroom staring intently into the mirror of the large oak dresser.

"Stella, you so much has happened to me over the course of the past seventy years, I never thought I'd live to see seventy. So much has happened between us. I never thought we'd still be married. Honey, I know I've done some things in the marriage I shouldn't have, but I'm glad to know you're still willing to celebrate my birthday with me. I can trust you. You know how important trust is to me."

Stella approached Boss and started tying his tie. "Joseph, honey, we've been married a little over fifty years and I don't regret one minute of my life with you. I love you and *only* you. You're a good man. I wish everyone could see that like I do."

"You mean everyone like Jesse Garmini?"

"Exactly. He still thinks you had his brother killed."

"Yeah, he thinks that because he had my younger brother killed. It still eats away at me."

"Honey, we can't prove he killed Sam just like Garmini can't prove you killed his brother."

Boss stared at the floor. The pain of his brother's death spread like wildfire throughout his body. "I killed no one and I had no one killed." His face became flush as he bellowed out the words.

Stella put her arms around Joseph, placing her head on his chest. "Oh, Honey, I believe you," she whispered softly.

"I really want to put all of this behind us. I have so many regrets."

"And we can. I'll figure something out later. But I want this day to be a celebration of *your* life. Now hurry up and let's go. You know our sons can't be left alone in a room together for too long. God only knows what could happen."

Boss and Stella arrived at the United Continental Suites Hotel about fifteen minutes late for the birthday party. As they entered the lobby, Ralph was standing there waiting to greet them. "I was getting a little nervous. You two are always early."

"We were having a discussion which lasted a little longer than expected," replied Boss as he lightly patted Ralph on his cheek.

"Well, it was worth the wait. You guys look terrific. Ma, I love your royal blue dress. Those beads around the neckline really add class. Dad, you always wear a tux with such style. I'm proud to be able to tell anyone that you are my parents."

"You know Donna Karan always did suit me well," joked Stella while pecking her eldest son on both his cheeks. Of all her children, she felt closest to Ralph. She knew if anything ever happened to Joseph, Ralph would make sure she was well taken care of. "You can't imagine how proud we are of you, son." Stella's voice quivered as she spoke. "Now let's get to the party."

Ralph escorted his parents to the left side of the lobby for Joseph's birthday celebration.

Ovasta and Vince pulled in front of the exquisite United Continental Suites Hotel for the Director's Inauguration Ball. A valet met them at the hotel entrance and opened the door for Vince. "Take care of my baby," said Vince as he tapped the side of his silver Lexus ISC.

"Yes, sir!" exclaimed the valet after Vince handed him the keys.

Vince sauntered around the car and opened the door for Ovasta. He spoke in an Old English accent as he reached down to grab her hand. "May I have your hand, my lady?"

"Why, certainly, my lord." Ovasta giggled, mimicking the same accent.

"Did I tell you that you look like royalty?" Vince asked, commenting on her beautiful red satin Oscar de la Renta evening gown.

"You did, but I wouldn't mind hearing it again. Did I tell you that you're the sexiest man alive, especially in that Armani tux?"

"Yes, you did. But please tell *People* magazine. You know I didn't even make their list this year."

Arm in arm, they entered into the hotel lobby laughing. Phillip was standing in the lobby near the information desk along with Laura, a hotel employee.

"Hello, you two. I hear congratulations are in order," said Phillip upon seeing the couple.

"Thanks. Yes, they are. News certainly travels fast," replied Vince.

Phillip chuckled as he held his hand out in order to shake Vince's hand. He looked at Ovasta. "Ovasta, you are looking as beautiful as ever. I look forward to hearing your speech tonight."

"Thank you, Phillip. I appreciate it."

Phillip pointed towards the right side of the lobby. "Our dinner party is this way. There's another party in the left wing of the hotel."

"It must be someone very important because I saw at least four limos outside," replied Vince.

"Do you know who they are?" Phillip asked Laura who was still at the desk.

"It's a party for the Stacolli family."

"The *who* family?" queried Phillip.

Laura pursed her lips at Phillip. "The Stacolli family. I'm surprised there is anybody in this city who hasn't heard of the Stacolli family."

Vince shook his head. "I'll confess that I've never heard of them either."

"Same here," stated Ovasta.

"I don't read the gossip column," Phillip replied curtly.

"For the record, it's not gossip," rebutted Laura. "They've done a lot of good things for this city. They've built youth centers. They donate used cars to veterans. Also, Mr. Stacolli's mother died of breast cancer so he's donated plenty of money to the hospital for cancer research."

"Humph. Interesting. I probably should go and meet him. Maybe he could attend the board meetings and become a more integral part of the hospital's agenda. What do you think, Ovasta?" questioned Phillip.

"It might be worth a shot. Who knows?"

Laura interrupted the conversation. "I doubt they'd let a stranger into Mr. Stacolli's party. He's got plenty of security. You should be very careful." Laura's brows lowered, creating several frown lines.

"I'm going to go and take a peak, so I'll catch up with the two of you later."

Ovasta and Vince gladly turned away from Phillip as he walked towards the other dining hall. It was always so hard thinking of things to say to him.

"He seemed rather pleasant today, didn't he?" asked Ovasta.

"Yes, maybe he's gotten over the fact that you were elected as board president instead of him."

Ovasta shrugged her shoulders. "I can't afford to worry about him. I've got some big shoes to fill."

Tenderly, Vince gazed at her. "Not really. You'll make a new path just as Mr. Gerard did with his predecessor. Adding your own style and creative methods to further the hospital's mission to provide the best care possible for its patients and their families."

Ovasta's eyes filled with tears ready to shed at a moment's notice. "Thank you for that, honey. I'm so grateful to have someone like you in my life."

"I'm glad to be a part of your life. I'm so proud of you." Vince pecked her on the lips then glanced into the banquet hall. "Hey, we better get inside. I see Mr. Gerard waving at us."

"Well, I know Riya is. She's been texting me for the past half hour."

Upon entering the dining room, time flew by very quickly. Before she knew it, Ovasta was on the podium and had all but completed her speech when she eyed Phillip entering the door and sitting at a table in the back of the room. *Never mind him. My speech has been well received by the people who really matter in my life,* she thought as she cleared her throat and spoke her final words. "Lastly, let me say how honored I am to be the newly-elected board president. I am truly grateful to all those who supported me, especially Mr. Gerard, his wife Tonya, my best friend Riya, and most certainly my fiancé Vince. Now let's eat! I've eaten little to nothing for the past couple of weeks in order to fit in this dress and I'm starving," Ovasta gave the audience a chortle while lightly placing both of her hands on her abdomen. "Thanks again, everyone."

The audience's laughter ran through the room as Ovasta left the podium. Vince helped her down the stairs and escorted her back to the table.

"That was absolutely wonderful, Ovasta!" exclaimed Gerard as she was being seated.

"Thank you, sir. You know none of this would be possible if it weren't for your guidance and support."

"Tonya and I are so pleased to see you take over this position. I'm sure you will do just fine. Plus, you have Vince who will continue to be a great support to you. Vince, you're a good man and a fine surgeon."

"Thank you, sir. It's been a pleasure to work with you as well."

Gerard nodded his head at Vince. "Alright, here comes the waiter with our salads. It's time to stop all of this talking and start enjoying our meal."

Chuckles filled the air. Ovasta grabbed a warm roll from the basket in front of her, then passed it to Riya. As she was eating, she glanced around, observing the banquet hall in awe. The room was exquisite, vaulted walls with one of the largest etched glass chandeliers she had ever seen hovering over the wooden floor which was designated for dancing. The table was decorated with white tablecloths, black napkins, and a black-rimmed pattern on the china. The covered chairs at each table alternated between black and white satin fabric with a large bow made of nylon tulle ribbon tied on the back. Glass tubular vases containing black and white floral arrangements served as centerpieces. Their fresh fragrance furthered the elegant ambience.

"Don't you think this ballroom is lovely?" Ovasta directed her question to everyone at the table. "I was so fixated on making my speech that I didn't even notice it."

"It is a very nice room," replied Vince while glancing around. "I didn't notice it because I was so fixated on you," he said seductively.

She smiled. "Thank you, Vince. You're the sweetest man I know." Ovasta glanced at Vince. Powerless, her eyes instantly pulled into his.

"You two are so inspiring," commented Mrs. Gerard, eyeing the newly-engaged couple. "True love is so hard to find. And when you do find it, never let it go."

"That's the plan," Vince responded. "'Til death do us part."

As Vince was speaking, the waiter came to the table with the evening meal. The aroma of brisket of beef, baked rosemary–lemon chicken, mashed garlic red potatoes, and green bean amandine flowed into the air mingling with the merriment of the occasion.

After dinner, the DJ announced dancing would begin. Ovasta and Vince headed to the dance floor.

He whispered in her ear as they began to slow dance. "I wish this song would never end and I never had to let you go."

She laid her head on his shoulder. The smell of his cologne titillated her senses, eventually tugging at her heartstrings. "The song may end but we won't. I didn't even know I was incomplete until I met you."

Vince exhaled deeply, gently drawing her closer.

Towards the song's end, the DJ announced there would be line dancing led by Riya Davison. Riya had briefly taught line dancing and Zumba prior to becoming the hospital's head nurse. Even Mr. and Mrs. Gerard participated in the Cupid Shuffle.

"This is the most fun I've had in a long time," Gerard exclaimed as he waddled to the left, next to Vince.

"I'm glad to see you're enjoying yourself, sir," responded Vince as his pager rumbled in his pocket. Vince turned to Ovasta. "I believe the hospital's calling. There must be some kind of emergency. I'll be right back."

"Okay," replied Ovasta happily as she turned to the right with the music.

After a few moments, Vince walked rapidly to the dance floor approaching Ovasta. "I'm going to have to leave. I've just been told there's an accident on the highway. Plenty of people in the ER. Some with brain trauma. They need all the help they can get." Vince appeared determined, his shoulders slightly slumped, with downcast eyes and tightened lips.

"Don't worry about me. Duty calls. Riya can take me home. Those poor souls definitely need your help."

"I'm glad you understand. I'll see you later." Vince quickly kissed Ovasta and rushed swiftly out of the ballroom going past Phillip as he went out the door.

"Hey, Ovasta, what's going on with Vince?" inquired Phillip as he sauntered in her direction.

"Some type of emergency at the hospital."

"Well, if you need a ride home, don't hesitate to ask."

"Thank you for the offer, Phillip. I'm genuinely touched." Ovasta stared at Phillip standing there in his black tux and bow tie. "You really look nice tonight. I should have told you that earlier."

Phillip's eyes widened in surprise behind his glasses. "Thanks for the compliment. I appreciate it." He strode away the moment he noticed Riya coming near them.

"What did he want?" questioned Riya, glowering.

"Oddly enough, he saw Vince leave and offered to take me home if I needed a ride."

Riya drew closer. "Oh, I didn't see Vince leave. Is everything alright?"

"Some type of emergency at the hospital."

"Sorry to hear that. I hate to say this but I'm going to have to leave as well. It's almost midnight and I have an early shift tomorrow. I don't usually work on Saturdays, but one of the other nurses had to travel out of town to see about her mother who is very ill. I dread even thinking this but would you feel safe riding with Phillip?" Riya glanced furtively towards the back of the room where Phillip was standing talking to Samuel King.

"Phillip's been surprisingly civil tonight. I think I'll take him up on his offer because I don't want to leave right now. There are a couple of guests I haven't had a chance to personally thank for coming tonight."

"Well, I guess this really is a new chapter in your life. Being on good terms with Phillip. Who would've thought? Anyway, congratulations, again. This was so much fun! I have lots of pictures. Maybe we can look at them tomorrow.

I'll see you later. Smooches." Riya and Ovasta exchanged air kisses.

Riya snickered as she headed out of the ballroom door. Ovasta saw Phillip across the room. Using her index finger she pointed to herself and mouthed the words, "Can I ride home with you?"

Phillip grinned, giving her a thumbs-up. Ovasta made her way around the room, offering sincere thanks to all who joined her in the celebration.

Some time had passed when Phillip approached Ovasta smiling. "Ovasta, there are only three guests left and they're leaving. I think we can go home now," he laughed.

She realized it was the first time she had heard his laugh in years. "You're right and it is almost twelve thirty. I guess if we stay any longer, they'll ask us to clean up."

"No. They're used to late-night parties. Also, I went down the hall to go to the restroom. It sounded like the people in the other room were still going strong."

"Well, I'm going home. Thanks again for offering to take me."

"No problem." Phillip pulled his valet ticket out of his pocket. "I'm going to get my car and I'll meet you out front."

"Okay, see you in a few minutes."

Although tired from the long day, Ovasta's heart was flooded with joy at the thought of finally reconciling with Phillip. Maybe they could work in tandem together once again. She didn't want to get her hopes up too high, opting to downplay her feelings as a defense mechanism. She strolled out of the ballroom waving goodbye to the waiters and waitresses who were cleaning up the tables. Even briefly chatting with Laura who was still at the front desk. Afterwards, she went outside and stood next to Phillip who was still waiting for the valet to bring his car.

At the same time the people at Board of Director's ball were eating, Boss and the Stacolli clan had just finished their chicken parmesan, braciole, orzo with fontina and peas, and fettuccini alfredo which were all of Boss's favorite dishes. As part of the festivities, Ralph invited dancers to perform the Tarantella for his father. Boss sat happily at the head table with Stella by his side along with Ralph, and his wife and Solomon Trimm, a city councilman and his wife, Vivian.

"I love these dancers!" exclaimed Boss, clapping to the music's fast beat.

"I knew you would. I saw them perform last year and immediately thought of you. They moved their schedules around so they could be here." Ralph watched his father. He was elated to see him in such high spirits.

As the dancers finished, Patrick went to the podium. "I hope everyone has truly enjoyed themselves. My brothers and I would like to thank everyone for coming. It's so good to see over one hundred guests in attendance considering it was such short notice. On behalf of the family, I'd like to say thank you again. Now, I'd like to dedicate the first song to my parents, Joseph and Stella Stacolli."

Lively applause ensued as Frank Sinatra's voice permeated the room. Boss stood up. "Dance with me."

Stella beheld her husband standing near her. His hand outstretched. Irresistible. She got up nearly falling into his arms. He twirled her around once and then held her close, serenading her, his raspy voice tingling her ear. Once Boss stopped singing, the pair snickered joyously like two children in a toy store. After a few moments of looking on, their guests joined them on the dance floor.

"Hey, Grandpa, Grandma, can we play something a little more up to date?" exclaimed Junnie from across the room as the song was coming to an end.

"Sure, go ahead and play that Taylor woman you like to hear. You know, the one who sings 'Shake It Up'," replied Boss as he twisted his waistline, causing his belly to wobble.

"Grandpa, it's 'Shake It *Off*'," laughed Junnie as he approached his grandparents.

"Up or off, I'm going to sit down." Joseph merrily strode back to his table.

"Come on, Grandma, dance with me." Junnie grabbed Stella's hands moving them up and then down to the beat which was now playing in the background.

Stella bobbed her head and body from side to side, occasionally moving her feet to the music's rhythm. Her eyes appeared to dance as well, while her broadened smile exposed most of her teeth. All the children gathered around Stella, excited to jump and dance with their grandmother.

Several songs had passed when James Williams approached Junnie. Williams, with his Lou Ferrigno physique, was the head of the family's security team. "Hey, it's getting late. How about I take you home? Most of your cousins are leaving now, too."

"Okay, thanks. I really do need to leave. I have a long day tomorrow."

Junnie sauntered over to his parents. "Dad, our security guards volunteered to take me home," said Junnie to his parents, standing in front of them with Williams.

"No problem, son, I know Williams will take good care of you. Don't forget to tell your grandparents good night," instructed Ralph.

"Okay. See you later." Junnie ambled over to Boss and Stella's table. "Grandma, Grandpa, I'm leaving with Williams. I need to get a good night's sleep. I have to take the ACT test in the morning and it's already well after midnight."

"ACT, you trying to get into college early?" questioned Joseph while putting his shot glass on the table.

"It's a practice test which you can take in your junior year. Hopefully, I'll score high enough that I won't need to take it again."

"I know you'll do well, grandson. You're the smartest kid I know. I love you. We both do."

Junnie leaned forward. Joseph grabbed the sides of Junnie's face, his coarse plump hands pulling it in a downward motion. He kissed the top of his grandson's head. "Good night, son. Sweet dreams."

"Goodnight, Grandpa, Grandma." Junnie ran over to Stella giving her a quick peck on the cheek.

Stella kissed Junnie on his cheek. "I forgot to tell you how handsome you look all dressed up. And you know I always like it when your hair is gelled backwards. It accentuates your handsome face."

"Thanks, Grandma," giggled Junnie as Stella pinched his now reddened face.

Boss and Stella waved as Junnie, Williams, and two other security members, Albert Stokes and James Jones, left the ballroom.

Once outside, Junnie and Williams stood next to Ovasta and Phillip in front of the hotel while the other two security guards went to get the limousine.

Ovasta turned and spoke, "Hello, young man. How are you doing tonight?" she queried.

"Fine, ma'am, how are you?"

"I'm good. Thanks for asking." Ovasta smiled and started to say something else.

Phillip interrupted her. "I wonder what's taking the valet so long to bring my car?" said Phillip, interrupting Ovasta's small talk with Junnie. "Wait here, Ovasta, I'm going to see what's going on."

"Sure, no problem. I may step inside because it's starting to get cold."

"Okay. If I don't see you I'll blow my horn and you can come on out."

Phillip ran through the hotel's parking lot, disappearing in the distance. Ovasta was getting colder by the minute. Goosebumps began to form on her arms and legs. As soon as she decided to go back inside the hotel lobby, a black limousine pulled up along the curb beside where she was standing.

"Get in," demanded the voice in the limo.

Junnie strolled aimlessly over to his grandfather's limo.

"He meant you, too," snarled Williams to Ovasta in a low tone.

Ovasta glared at him, perplexed. She pointed her finger at her chest. "Me?"

"Yeah, you know the drill, get in."

"Sir, you must have me mixed up with somebody else. I already have a ride but thank you anyway." Ovasta swiftly turned attempting to head towards the hotel lobby. Williams gripped her arm squeezing it tightly. "I don't know what your problem is but you're going with us."

"What in the world are you talking about? Let me go." Ovasta tried to jerk away. Williams' grip got tighter. Fear ran through her heart. He pushed her inside the back seat of the limo next to Junnie who fixated his glare on her, noticing the terror in her eyes.

"Guys, what are you doing? Who is this woman? You know Grandad doesn't allow people he doesn't know in his limo."

"What are you talking about? You may not know who she is but that doesn't mean Boss doesn't," replied Williams angrily.

Ovasta shook her head from side to side. "I don't know anyone named Boss. I want to get out now. This must be some type of mistake." Trembling with fear, Ovasta was barely able to get the words out.

Williams got in the back seat next to Ovasta, shoving her closer to Junnie. The smell of Williams's cheap cologne penetrated her nostrils, causing them to contract.

"Junnie, you'll find out in about one minute what's going on," laughed Williams, Stokes, and Jones mockingly.

"Okay, we're here," announced Jones from the front passenger seat as Stokes pulled the car around the back of the hotel near the dumpsters.

Junnie protested. "What do you mean we're '*here*?' My dad thinks you're taking me home. So do my grandparents. If they ever find out—"

Williams briskly leaned his muscular body across Ovasta, putting the palm of his huge hand within one inch of Junnie's face. His hot breath singed her skin. "They never will if you know what's good for you. Remember, we know all your family's dirty little secrets. We even know who's on the take at the police department. You tell what happens tonight and we'll make sure that everything we know goes public. Now get out of the car!"

Junnie opened the limo door, his stomach tied up in knots. He slid across the leather seat placing his black patent leather shoes on the muddy ground.

Williams turned to Ovasta, leering. "Now,you . . .get out!" his blue eyes scanned Ovasta's body like an X-ray machine, making the hairs on her body stand at attention.

Swiftly, she got out of the car to escape his glare. After giving each other a once-over, she and Junnie stared at the security team who now stood directly in front of them leering.

"Tonight is your night, Junnie, and this beautiful little lady right here is going to help make a man out of you," snarled Williams.

"What do you mean? I have no idea what you're talking about." Junnie's heart skipped a beat, then started to race.

"The Stacollis can't afford to have any gays in the family. They got a reputation to uphold. So, we figured if you ever got the taste of a real woman, you'd never even think about a man."

Tears rolled down Junnie's cheeks. He struggled to keep his food down as his stomach started to cramp. "What? Who said I was even thinking about anybody. Please, Williams, I . . . I . . . just want to go home. I'll do anything you ask. If you want more money, I can ask my dad or grandfather to give it to you. If you need more time off, we can figure something out. But don't do this. Please take me home."

Ovasta's knees got weak as she saw the young man pleading. At this point, she had no idea what to do. She glanced around to see if there was any way to escape.

"Boy! Stop your whining and shut your trap. You'll thank me later." Williams noticed Ovasta's eyes intensely moving back and forth. He scolded her. "What are you searching for? Get down on the ground on your back." Williams pulled his suit jacket back, exposing a holster with a gun in it.

Ovasta complied, kneeling gradually. The stench of garbage from the dumpster filled her nose. The cold moist ground caused a shiver to run down her spine. She turned her head away from Williams and Stokes.

I can't believe this is happening, she thought. *Where's*

Phillip? I wonder if he's looking for me. My purse is in that limo. Maybe he called me. I hope he didn't leave thinking I'd found another ride. I pray he finds me. God please let him find me. She braced herself for what was next. Her body stiffened.

Williams frowned. He squinted at Jones and Stokes. "I don't understand what's going on with her. She knows the deal."

"I bet that creep didn't even pay her," replied Stokes.

"Yeah, I never did like him. He rubs me the wrong way," growled Jones.

"You guys are probably right. Don't worry, honey. We'll take care of you. Hey Jones, check the hotel door and make sure no one is coming. I don't want any witnesses." Jones walked past the dumpster near the back entrance of the hotel.

Ovasta wondered what they were talking about. *What deal? Who was the creep?* She knew they had the wrong person. She sat up opening her mouth to say something. Anything to explain to them that she wasn't the person they were expecting.

"Get back on the ground," Williams commanded as soon as he saw her move while pulling the gun out of the holster. Williams glared at Junnie. "You said you'd do anything. Pull your pants down, boy, and let's get this over with."

"*No!* I won't do it. I'm not touching her." Junnie pointed on the ground where Ovasta lay face up. Eyes staring blankly into space.

"I don't want to hurt you 'cuz you're Boss' grandson. But I will if I have to." Williams sauntered over to Junnie. *Whack.* Junnie's head jerked forward from Williams' swift blow to the back of his head.

The noise caused Ovasta to whip her head around. She saw Junnie grimace, putting his hand on his neck.

"Williams!" yelled Stokes. "You can't afford to leave any bruises on the boy. If Boss ever sees them and even *thinks* we had anything to do with it . . . Stokes paused, breathing heavily, running his hands through his curly dark-brown hair. "He'll kill us and our entire families." Stokes began pacing back and forth, his head held down.

"Stokes, stop your whining. I'm a professional. I don't leave bruises. We can make it seem like an accident and no one will ever know. Not even Boss." Williams' cocky grin infiltrated the atmosphere. He turned away from Stokes, speaking directly into Junnie's ear. "Did you hear that, boy? Now pull your pants down." Junnie, paralyzed with fear, did not move. "Do you need help?" Williams reached for Junnie's belt buckle.

Junnie jerked away. "Don't touch me. I can do this myself."

"I'm surprised you don't want me to touch you there," Williams said sarcastically. "I thought that's what you liked. Looks like you're manning up already."

Junnie unclasped his belt, then unzipped his pants, his hands trembling. His gaze fixed on the ground beside Ovasta. He couldn't bear to allow their eyes to meet. He sobbed. "I'm so sorry, ma'am. I'm so sorry."

With a motionless body, Junnie sat in the back of the limo as Jones drove him home. His mind, however, was caught in a tailspin. Spinning relentlessly as he attempted to comprehend what happened. He couldn't grasp it. How could they do this to him? What had he done to deserve such treatment? He knew Williams never liked him, but this was extreme. Uncalled for. Both numbness and nausea assaulted his body. Blood rushed to his face. Sweat engulfed him. How could he face his family and friends after what had occurred only moments ago? And that poor woman. Who was she? He'd never seen her before. There was no way she was working with Williams. Yet, Williams kept speaking to her like she should know what was going on. Talking about a deal and some creep. What was that about? He had no way of knowing. But the fear in the woman's eyes and the stiffness of her body spoke more than words ever could. Tale tail signs that she was as bewildered as he. Junnie cringed inside at the thought of her. At the thought of having touched her. Knowing neither of them wanted this to happen. And even as they were leaving, after the damage had been done, the horrible image of her lying on the ground rolled around in his mind. Seeing the dirt and mud absorb into her black hair and beautiful red dress. Although an unwilling participant, he hated himself for being a part of it and he couldn't believe they left her there. Alone. It was horrible. Absolutely horrible.

To make matters worse, he was threatened by Williams

all the way home. All Junnie could see was Williams's fore-finger being jabbed in his face. His hot breath fogged the limo's windows. The stench of his cologne wafted in the air. At one point, spittle even expelled from his mouth, as he spewed out insults and curse words. Soiling parts of Junnie's face. Angrily, Williams exclaimed that if Boss ever found out what happened, he'd be killed for helping to orchestrate it. But he offered Junnie a strong warning. He stated he had secret files and records. Things that would put Junnie's father and grandfather in prison for life. Or, even possibly cause them to get the death penalty. Should Williams die and untimely death, someone had been paid to send all the information to the police.

Albeit he had never seen his father or grandfather harm anyone, Junnie knew his family had a hand in the death of at least one person. Junnie recalled that when he was about eight years old, he and his cousins were playing in the back-yard. He grew thirsty and decided to go into the house for a glass of lemonade. As he neared the door, he heard gran-dad speaking in hushed tones to his father, Williams, and Jones. Grandad sounded angry. He wasn't one to raise his voice. Instead, it grew deeper and deeper with each word. Wondering what was going on, Junnie leaned up against the outside of the house and put his ear near the door barely out of their view. Granddad said that one of his employees at the car dealership, David Haddon, was stealing money and falsifying accounts. Haddon sold the cars for more than he actually reported, then pocketed the difference. Granddad instructed Williams to get rid of him because this wasn't the first time he'd done something the family didn't like. He had been warned, Grandad said and now it was time to pay.

At the time, Junnie thought "get rid of him" meant the man was going to be fired. But two days later, Junnie saw on the news he'd been killed. The police found Haddon's body in a ditch not too far from his home. Someone had shot him in the head. Junnie didn't want to believe his father or grandfather had anything to do with it. Especially since a week later, most of the family attended the funeral. But deep down he still felt his family was involved. There had been plenty of whispering between Williams, Grandad, and his father in the days following and he heard Haddon's name mentioned several times.

Of course, Junnie had no real proof. He never actually witnessed anything. However, if anyone did have proof, it would be Williams. He had a hand in everything that was going on with the Stacolli family and was with Granddad most of the time. There was no way Junnie was going to tell. He couldn't risk both his father and grandfather going to jail. The family couldn't survive without them.

Williams' hostility followed Junnie as he exited the limo and went inside his home after what appeared to be an endless ride. At a feverish pace, he dashed up spiral staircase trying to escape the events of the night.

On the wall of the landing, was a picture of his parents standing while hugging one another and smiling from ear to ear into the camera. He'd always loved the picture. Although his father was much larger than his mother, she was always able to calm the fierce anger which seemed to rage within him. It was almost like beauty and the beast, however, he didn't quite view his father that way. Dad had a gentleness his mother was able to bring to the surface like no other. He was her Sugar Bear. She was his Peaches. They loved each other. They loved him and the smile on their faces in the picture was enough to light up the room.

Today, however, he could barely look at either of them. Ashamed, he swiftly turned away and dashed down the long hallway to his bedroom, pulled off all of his clothing, rolled them into a ball, and tossed them angrily into the wastebasket. He grabbed a cotton bathrobe out of his closet and wrapped it swiftly around his shivering body.

Not wanting any remnant of *her* to be in his bedroom, he went to the guest room down the hall and took a shower. *Her.* He didn't even know her name. How sad it was for both of them. It wasn't supposed to be that way. All his thoughts and dreams about what love should be were crushed by Williams. Williams made it dirty and disdainful. Horrid. Junnie felt like he was going to hyperventilate.

He jumped in the shower and turned the water on as hot as he could possibly stand it, hoping it would wash away the pain he felt in his heart. After several minutes of standing there letting the water roll off his body, he started to weep. He fell against the white ceramic tile of the shower wall and slid down slowly until he hit the tub. Briefly, he considered putting his head under the running water in an attempt to end the current pain and suffering. He shook himself, mustarding up some strength. *No. I'm a Stacolli. We don't give up. We get even.* Anger rushed through his veins as the water drenched his hair and clouded his vision. Slowly, he rose up and grabbed a bar of soap from the holder which hung from the shower head. He got a washcloth from the towel rack right outside the shower. He scrubbed his skin hard attempting to remove any traces of tonight from his skin.

After showering, he put on his robe and ran back down the hall to his room shutting the door hard behind him. Briefly, he thought about calling Charles but didn't want to disturb him so late at night, opting instead to send him a text saying that he would not be taking the ACT as planned. He said he wasn't feeling well and would talk to Charles later. He put his phone on the charger then placed it upon the nightstand beside the bed. He crept across the room timidly to the light switch. Afraid to turn it off. He felt like a small child. Terrified to go to sleep for fear of monsters hiding under the bed. For a moment, he debated on whether or not to drink his problems away. It seemed to work for so many of his family members. He knew that his parents had plenty of wine. However, he couldn't make a trek to the cellar. The last thing he wanted right now was to be in a cold, dark place. With shaking hands, he turned off the light switch and jumped into bed. He lay on his back and stared upward into the dark abyss, praying for sleep.

Phillip pulled his royal blue Audi A7 to the hotel's entrance. Not seeing Ovasta, he began to blow his horn. To pass the time, he hit the power button on his car stereo. "Sure Got Cold After the Rain Fell" by ZZ Top played on the radio. A few minutes later he decided to go back into the hotel and look for her. *Maybe she got cold* he thought. He put the car in park, left his flashers on, and went back inside. There was no sign of her anywhere. He called her cell but no response. Unsure of what to do next, he drove cautiously around the hotel parking lot, turning his head from left to right. He headed towards the back, passing a black limousine. Phillip ignored the vehicle, scanning the parking lot for any signs of Ovasta. As he reached the back of the building, he saw a figure in the darkness lying on the ground near the dumpsters. Phillip sprang out of the car, leaving it running with the door open. "Oh, my God! Ovasta, is that you?" Almost tiptoeing, he approached the seemingly lifeless body with caution. "Ovasta? Please say something . . . *anything.*" Phillip's voice was filled with agony. He pulled his glasses off to wipe them as it had started to drizzle.

Gradually, deliberately, he knelt over her body searching for signs of life. Ovasta lay there. Back arched, chin burrowed in her chest, arms crossed around her abdomen, knees bent towards near her chest. Motionless. He heard a faint, weak voice.

"Take me home. I want to go home."

Phillip exhaled a sigh of relief. "Thank God," he whispered under his breath. "What happened?"

Ovasta collected enough strength to untangle her limbs. Her body unfolded like a time-lapse movie of a butterfly emerging from its cocoon. The drizzle grew heavier. Each raindrop pounded down on her skin. She sat up. Her body swayed back and forth like a drunken sailor. Phillip watched her, her red dress now brown with mud.

"Ovasta, you're in shock! You need to get checked out immediately! I'm going to call an ambulance!" Hurriedly, Phillip dialed 911. He sat down on the ground next to her until the ambulance came. He noticed several $100 bills approximately two feet away from Ovasta. He dared not ask her about the money. Since sitting up, she was speechless, only maintaining a cold, vacant stare. The ambulance arrived within ten minutes of the phone call. Phillip explained to them that he didn't know what happened. The EMS workers placed her on a gurney and put her in the back of the ambulance, taking her to the hospital where she worked. Phillip followed the ambulance, calling Vince on his Bluetooth while on his way to the emergency room. Vince's voicemail picked up. "Vince, this is Phillip. Something's happened to Ovasta. Meet us in the ER in about fifteen minutes." He hung up the phone abruptly, weaving in and out of traffic to keep up with the ambulance. Once they arrived at the hospital, Phillip phoned Vince again. This time Vince answered the phone.

"This is Phillip. Did you get my message?"

"No, I just got out of surgery. What's the problem?"

"It's Ovasta . . . something terrible has happened." Phillip's voice shuddered.

"What happened?" Vince's question bellowed through the phone.

"I'm not sure. I found her on the ground by a dumpster in the back of the hotel."

"*What!* What do you mean you're not sure? I thought she was with you. How could you let something happen to her? Where is she?" Vince's voice became more and more elevated with each question.

"She's in the ER," responded Phillip almost apologetically.

"I'm going to find Ovasta. I'll deal with you later."

The phone went dead. Phillip put his phone in his tux pocket and headed to the receptionist desk of the ER. By the time Vince got to the building's entrance, EMS workers had already wheeled Ovasta's gurney into an observation room.

"What's the problem?" he questioned one of the workers whom he'd seen around the hospital.

"I'm sorry, Dr. Parker but we think she's been sexually assaulted. The police have been called. They should be here any minute."

"Sexually . . . assaulted." Vince struggled to speak as he was breathing like an elephant was sitting on his chest.

"A nurse is with her now. It'll be a couple of minutes."

As soon as the nurse exited the room, Vince barged past the EMS worker and went inside the room. There she was, sitting up in the bed. Her beautiful red dress exchanged for a hospital gown. Her once swept-up hair now hanging down, tangled. No sparkle in her eye. No expression on her face. Zombie-like.

Vince wanted to touch her but knew better. "Ovasta, tell me how you're feeling right now. Is there anything I can do?"

Feeling the sympathy in his voice, she resolved not to look him in the eye. "I'm fine, Vince. I really want to go home but no one will take me. I want to put this day behind me and move on with my life." Ovasta's weak voice seemed to fade away at the end of the sentence.

"The police are here," announced one of the nurses.

Vince moved aside and let the officer in the room. "I'm her fiancé, Dr. Vince Parker."

"Hello, sir, I'm Officer Linda Daniels from the Rape Crisis Division. I'll need to question her and take some pictures. I believe a nurse has already done a complete forensic exam to collect evidence for later prosecution if the victim chooses to pursue legal action. It's probably better if you leave the room. She may not want you to hear all of the details," cautioned Daniels.

"I understand," Vince replied softly. He studied Ovasta who gazed blankly off into the distance. "Ovasta, if you want me to come in at any time, just call. I'll be standing outside the door." No response. Vince nearly stumbled out of the room as his head was spinning. Outside, he stood up straight like an army soldier, determined to remain calm although the earth felt as though it would crumble beneath his feet.

"Vince . . . *Vince.*" He heard Riya from a distance frantically calling his name, running down the hospital corridor like a tornado across the Great Plains. "Where's Ovasta? Is what I heard true? Tell me she wasn't harmed?" Riya reached out, grabbing Vince's arms, slightly shaking them. "Say something . . .*anything.*"

"It appears Ovasta was sexually assaulted. I don't know any more than that. The police are interviewing her right now."

"What? I thought she was with Phillip? Did he leave her stranded? I don't see how this could have happened." Riya covered her face with her hands, crying.

Vince put his arms around her. "Listen, we have to be strong for Ovasta. I need you to pull it together," he whispered softly. His smooth baritone voice pacified her.

"Okay." Riya lifted up her head, studying Vince's forced smile.

He dropped his arms from around her. "Now go and wipe your face. Running mascara is not a good look on you," he teased.

Riya forced a slight chuckle and shook her head with tears streaming down her face.

"We're going to find out who did this. But most of all we're going to help Ovasta get through it," continued Vince.

"I know we will. We don't have a choice. I'll be right back. I'm going to the ladies room." Riya turned, running down the hallway almost as quickly as she had arrived.

Officer Daniels came out of the room with a writing pad and pen in her hand. "She didn't give us much to go on. Only mentioning a black limo and four males."

"Four? Oh, my God!" Vince's heart froze.

Daniels rested her pudgy hand on his shoulder. "She was only assaulted by one person. It appears that the other three forced the fourth party. Almost like some type of initiation."

84

"Initiation? Was she able to describe any of the men?"

"Not really. Your fiancée is still in shock. I didn't want to traumatize her further with more questions at this time. I gave her my card and asked her to call me when she's feeling a little better. I want her to come down to the station and look through some mug shots to see if she can identify anyone. She was also given the number to a counseling center in her neighborhood. The good news is there are no bruises or any of the other types of injuries we usually see with rape victims. I'm sorry something like this had to happen to her. I wish you both well."

Vince shook her hand. She eyed him reflectively then turned away. Vince watched her as she marched down the hall. He was still in a state of disbelief over the night's current events.

SIX

I t had been four weeks since what Junnie deemed "the incident" had occurred. The day after, he had been unable to get out of bed in order to take the ACT as he had only gotten an hour of sleep. At that time, he told his parents he didn't feel well and they assumed it was because he stayed up too late for Boss' birthday celebration. Today, he was in his bedroom getting dressed, finally feeling well enough to take the test. Although some time had passed, sleep still evaded him. Promising to show up in the middle of the night only to be averted by terrible memories of what had been done to both he and the woman he'd been forced upon. The whole scenario ran rapidly in his mind. It made his skin crawl and left a putrid taste in his mouth.

Most of all he hated Williams for playing the main role in the horror show that plagued his thought life. Williams, who had come over to the house on several occasions under the pretense of checking on him because he'd heard Junnie was sick. When his parents turned their back, Williams would mouth the words, "Remember what I said." A scowl would cover his face. He recalled how one time his dad almost caught Williams threatening him, but Williams be-gan acted as if he was choking and the family housekeeper got him something to drink. Junnie cringed as he remem-bered the sly smile he was given as Williams drank the water down ever so slowly.

Petrified, Junnie began leaving any room whenever he saw Williams coming. But no matter how hard he tried, he couldn't escape. Williams even started picking Junnie up from school. Showing up at the library where he, Charles, and several of his other friends were studying. Harassing Junnie continuously. It seemed to never end.

Junnie couldn't understand his actions at all. His gran-dad trusted Williams more than any of the others who worked for the family. Maybe even more than his sons. Grandad probably would have done anything for him. Clearly, Williams didn't feel the same way. Nobody would purposely harm the family members of someone you claim to care about. It would tear grandad apart to know this was happening.

It had been a month since the rape. During that time, Ovasta left the house only once, taking a trip to the police station followed by a visit to the doctor's office. Most days were spent in pajamas, sitting on the floor in front of the television with Major and watching the Lifetime channel. Vince and Riya visited her every day, ensuring she ate at least one meal as she was experiencing a loss of appetite.

At times they thought she appeared almost "normal" until she'd abruptly erupt into fits of crying. Vince told her some people think they can get over traumatic events alone or that time will heal them. "But those events are like diseases. If not treated, they do not go away. They get worse," he said, finally convincing her to seek professional help.

Ovasta met with Mrs. Janice Lions, a rape counselor who encouraged her to go back to work after they had had several sessions together. While they discussed her return, she contemplated how hard it would be to face her colleagues. Awkward silences. Forced smiles. Sympathetic stares. Simply envisioning it made her skittish. Lions suggested she deal with it one day at a time as this needed to be done if she wanted to gain control of her life.

Once home, Ovasta elected to tell Vince of her intended return to work. There was a brief hesitation after she pulled her cell phone out of her purse. Having not dialed out in the past month, it took a few seconds to recall the cell's passcode. She snickered at the thought of not remembering it. However, it soon reminded her of how isolated she'd become. Consequently, the snicker was met with a tear which inadvertently rolled down her cheek. Ovasta inhaled deeply, gathering the impending outburst into her lungs and exhaling it out into the air like Old Man Winter sending a blast of arctic air in the wintertime. *Better. Not great, but better.* Dialing, she called Vince.

"Ovasta?" There was surprise in his voice.

"Yes. It's me. I wanted to tell you something." She hesitated as if waiting for a drum roll. "At the advice of my counselor, I'm coming back to work." In her voice, there was a hint of excitement and hope.

"I can't tell you how glad I am to hear those words!" He paused for a moment. "Do you feel you're ready?" he continued delicately.

"As ready as I'll ever be."

"Do you mind if I come over tonight and bring you dinner?"

"Haven't you and Riya been doing that for the past month?"

Vince sighed at her sarcastic tone. "I know. We did it because we were so concerned about you. Because we both love you. *I* love you. But I don't want to force the issue anymore. I need you to want to see me."

Ovasta did not respond immediately. She began to pace back and forth across the floor. "I'd like you to come. See you later?" Her soft voice, reminiscent of old times.

"See you later."

Vince hung up the phone. Ovasta knew he loved her but was unsure how she felt at this juncture in her life. She trusted Vince. Nonetheless, unfounded fears flooded her heart. Determined not to focus on the negative, she chose to take Major out for a midday stroll.

"Go get your leash, boy." Major jumped up, going to the kitchen where the leash was hanging from a wooden rod on the wall next to the back door. Ovasta smiled as she headed to her room to change. No matter how many times she'd seen it, Major continued to amaze her by sliding the leash off with his mouth and bringing it to her. Before she had taken off her clothes, he pranced to her bedroom, dropped the leash on the bed next to where she was sitting, and sat down, waiting for her to finish getting dressed. "Good boy!" she exclaimed, patting his head. Ovasta was putting on a blue sweat suit and white Reebok tennis shoes.

Once dressed, Ovasta picked the leash up off her pale blue down comforter and put it around his neck. Major scurried out of the bedroom, brown paws sliding across the wooden floor to the door. Ovasta gently pulled the leash back, reducing his speed. "Calm down, Major. I know it's been a long time since we went on a walk." Ovasta laughed. The almost foreign sound pushed memories of happier times to the forefront of her mind. She clutched the brass doorknob, pulling it open gradually. *I can do this. I really can.* The open door ushered in a chilly north wind which swept her face. "We'll make this a short walk, Major. I'm cold already." Major romped out of the house down the street like he was competing in the Westminster Dog Show. His black tail extended, giving him a longer leaner appearance.

While strolling through the neighborhood, they passed various intricately detailed Victorian-style homes with regal trim work and designs full of history. Ovasta had driven down this street many times never noticing them. Snowflakes filled the air as they reached the last home at the end of the street. Major led the way making a left turn onto the main street. The contrast between the side street and the main one was striking. Filled with people, restaurants, bars, and even a psychic or two, it was like traveling from a faraway land to New York City in less than a heart-beat. Ovasta struggled to keep her composure as a teenaged male accompanied by two thirtysomething-year-old males approached her. *Definitely not them. They look nothing like them. No need to panic.* After eyeing them cautiously, she eased past them, grateful for the ability to remain calm. Spotting a coffee shop down the street, she decided to get some coffee and pastries for the walk home. She left Major tied outside while she went in, purchasing hazelnut coffee, a few scones, and three glazed doughnuts, buying a little extra to share with Vince and Riya.

Ambling back outside, the hazelnut aroma released a small portion of tension from her body. Sipping the warm brew helped further the calming effects. Ovasta grabbed Major's now snow-covered leash. "Okay, boy, just a little further and then we'll turn away and head home." At the end of the building which housed the coffee shop was an alley. Ovasta glanced down to ensure there was no traffic approaching. She noticed a dumpster near the alley's end. The sight of it stopped her in her tracks. Major stopped as well, his leash being tugged backwards. Visions of the attack flooded her mind. Although the dumpster was too far away, she swore she could smell it. Thoughts began to overwhelm her. The horrors of the attack plagued her dreams. Afraid to fall asleep. Too tired to stay awake. The words *"I'm sorry, I'm so sorry"* rang in her head, making her heart sink like the Titanic in the icy waters of the North Atlantic Ocean. *I don't understand why this happened to me. How could this have happened to me?* Panic set in.

The snowflakes burned her skin just as the raindrops did on that wretched night. Unable to move. Her feet were like lead. *Breathe. Breathe.* The rapid shallow breaths only made her heart race. Major started to bark, then whimper. He sat right in front of her, ears erect, waiting for her command. "We're going home, boy." Ovasta turned swiftly, accidentally dropping her coffee cup. *Why didn't I try to run from them? What could I have done differently?* She ran away as fast as she could. Major increased his stride beyond her capacity to keep up. Finally, Ovasta stopped, bent forward, placing her hands on her knees, chin near her chest, gasping, cold air filling her lungs. After catching her breath, she jogged briskly to the house. *At least I'm still alive. Grateful to be alive.*

SEVEN

Petrified. That's the way Ovasta felt on the first day back to work after being away for three weeks. Traveling from her townhouse to the hospital parking lot was like walking *The Green Mile*. Thoughts infiltrated her mind. *Am I ready for this? Can I handle it? Should I have waited a little longer?* She knew there was only one way to find out. By actually going to work. She believed the longer she stayed away, the harder it would be to return. Perseverance was the only way.

While in route, Ovasta listened to one of the CDs Mrs. Lions gave her after a counseling session, which contained several calming techniques. She brought a CD player and headphones from home to put on her desk with the intention of listening during breaks at work. Sluggishly entering the parking lot, she took a different route to her office to avoid seeing the other board members. Upon entering the office, she noticed a glass vase with a dozen red roses on the desk, the floral scent drawing her near. On the vase was a card which she decided to read a little later assuming it was from Vince. *He has to be the most thoughtful man I know.*

She smiled while hanging her black wool coat and scarf on the freestanding wooden coatrack which stood in the corner behind her desk. Rolling back the chair, she sat down slowly, wondering where to begin. There were sixty-five missed calls on the caller-ID and a stack of papers in the in-box on her desk. Frustrated. She sighed. *I can only do one thing at a time. Maybe I'll read the card first and then listen to the voicemails.*

> *I tried to contact you several times while you were out. I'm glad you're back. I'm here if you need me.*
>
> *Phillip.*

Surprised, Ovasta didn't know how she felt about the roses being from Phillip. True, he'd left several voice messages over the course of the past four weeks. But she never responded. His voice was a reminder of what happened. A painful memory she wasn't ready to deal with yet. She couldn't face him. The reality was part of her blamed him. If not for the delay in picking her up in front of the hotel lobby, those men wouldn't have had a chance to force her into the car. She thought he'd left her there as a joke. Making her wait on purpose. Or, maybe never even planning to pick her up, having a change of heart at the last minute. She began to pace the floor, never remembering rising from her desk. After several seconds, she collected her thoughts. Unsure what really happened, she decided to discuss it with him at a later date, choosing to face the problem head-on rather than living a life full of supposition. For right now, work awaited her.

Several people visited with Ovasta on her first day, mostly well-wishers who stopped by just to say, "Hello." Gerard met with her as well. He had been coming in three times a week to ensure things were running smoothly during her absence. Lindsay, his former assistant, kept him abreast of any pressing matters on a daily basis. As always, she was glad he was there. What a comforting presence he was. Like a loving father, he was one of the few people she didn't mind being around during this difficult time.

Towards the end of the day, Vince and Riya came to the office, the pair barely standing inside the door. Ovasta was still sitting at her desk when they arrived. Vince still in scrubs, Riya had exchanged her white nurse's uniform for a pair of blue jeans with a white button-down blouse and a gray blazer. Her gray Gucci belt accented her high-heeled shoes.

"Wow, you look great! What's the occasion?" Ovasta exclaimed when she saw Riya.

"Thanks. I have a dinner date tonight."

"With?"

"Orlando Harding."

Puzzled, Ovasta questioned her. "Isn't he the director of the nursing home your grandmother is in? Didn't he ask you out once before and you declined?"

"Yes. But my granny has nothing but good things to say about him. He seems like a really nice guy."

"Well, if he's not, he'll answer to us. I know some people

over there. I'll ask them to check him out," said Vince sincerely.

"I really wish you wouldn't. It's only one date." Riya smirked, rolling her eyes upward at Vince. "If later on I need your intermural spies, I'll let you know," she continued playfully.

"Okay," laughed Vince.

"Seriously, if things progress, maybe one day we can all have dinner together," stated Riya happily.

"Agreed," replied Vince and Ovasta in unison.

Riya stepped out of the doorway almost prancing, curls bouncing as she left.

"I haven't seen her this happy in a long time," noted Ovasta, beaming at her longtime friend as she left the office.

"I know. That last guy. What was his name? Harry, Larry, or was it scary? Anyway, I'm glad she kicked him to the curb."

"She had to. He was a liar and a con artist with a criminal record. As soon as she found out he'd been jailed for robbery and drug possession, she left him right at his momma's house."

Vince smiled. "And he presented so well. He probably stole that very nice suit I saw him wearing when we went out together." Vince turned earnest. "I don't want to talk about Riya anymore. Tell me, how are you holding up?"

"Pretty well, actually. When I first arrived, I wasn't sure I was going to be able to stay all day but then I had a long meeting with Mr. Gerard. He brought me up to speed on what's been going on here. He's so helpful . . . and understanding."

"Is that who gave you the roses?" Questioned Vince while smelling them, then sitting on the edge of the desk next to her chair.

"No. Actually, those came from Phillip. I believe they're a peace offering."

"Considering the circumstances, I'm going to overlook the roses. If there's ever a next time, I'll speak to Phillip myself. The odd thing is that I haven't seen him since the night of the Directors' Ball. I believe he was avoiding me. I actually went to his office on two different occasions but he wasn't there. You know there are a few people I wouldn't mind sending you roses. However, he's not one of them." Vince's chest expanded and his neck stiffened, generating considerable tension in the room.

"Vince." Ovasta lightly placed her hand on top of his, causing the tension to crash to the floor like a giant boulder falling from a cliff at Yosemite.

He eyed her intensely, careful not to touch her, embracing her with his eyes. She gradually withdrew her hand moving it at a downward angle across his skin. Her touch lingered in his senses for several moments.

"Tell me you love me," his Barry White-like voice chipped away at her fears.

"I do love you. I'm just afraid. I still have nightmares." Ovasta stared at the floor.

Vince put his thumb on her chin, lifting her head. "Can we go to my house? Sit down and eat a good meal. Maybe even watch a movie. Something funny, of course." Ovasta's voice straggled off as she shifted in her chair.

"Of course, sweetie. Of course. I'll catch up with you after work."

Ovasta smiled at him and watched as he walked out of the door. Her eyes started to tear. She was so grateful to have a patient, loving, and kindhearted man in her life. *I'll get through this. I absolutely have to for my sake and his.*

Ovasta spent the next couple of days in her office catching up on paperwork or returning phone calls, rarely venturing out with the exception of getting coffee or going to the restroom. Phillip put his head in the door on several occasions asking her if she needed assistance in any way. She thanked him for the flowers, suggesting a long conversation later in the week about what happened that night. Phillip agreed, appearing amenable to the idea.

By Friday, Ovasta felt particularly confident she could intermingle with colleagues in the employee lunchroom. Moving down the hospital corridor in a black pantsuit and flat shoes, she entered the lunchroom quietly. There were two tables, a refrigerator, a microwave on a wooden stand, and a couch all placed in one small room. Several people were in the room, but at first, she had gone unnoticed. Jacqueline Hanes, one of the newest board members, glanced up from her antipasti salad, seeing Ovasta in the corner of her eye retrieving lunch out of the refrigerator.

"Hey, Ovasta. It's good to see you out and about. Please, come, sit with us." Jacqueline appeared pleased to have Ovasta at their table, sporting a Cheshire grin on her chubby oval face, her brown eyes sparkling with glee through her bleach-blonde bangs in need of trimming. They had eaten together before but it was few and far between. She moved her lunch over to the side allowing space on the circular wooden table for Ovasta's chicken Cobb salad. Ovasta slid down into the white plastic lunchroom chair beside her, placing the salad on the table. Two other women were already seated prior to Ovasta's arrival. Although she had seen them in the hospital, she didn't know their names.

"Hello," said Ovasta politely.

"Hello," replied one of the women who favored Glenn Close. Both women moved closer to her, staring in awe. Ovasta was beginning to feel a little claustrophobic but decided to stay seated hoping it would pass. At the other table was one forty-something male and a female who appeared to be in her early fifties, neither of whom she recognized. They waved ecstatically like they'd known her forever, hands flapping like a dog with two tails. She waved back, attempting to match their excitement.

"I'm really looking forward to working with you and the rest of the board members. My family has known Mr. Gerard and his wife for a long time and he has had nothing but good things to say about you," stated Jacqueline as she pushed her bangs to one side, glancing at Ovasta.

"Thank you. No one could ever replace him but I have

some ideas that I believe will keep the hospital moving in a positive direction."

"If you need any help whatsoever, I'm a phone call away."

"Thanks, I plan to take you up on your offer."

The three women at the table ate happily while providing small talk. Ovasta listened quietly, not saying much of anything. Only furnishing a head nod or two. After about fifteen minutes, Jacqueline and the other two women excused themselves from the table as their lunch break was over. Shortly following, the two parties at the other table also cleared out, leaving Ovasta in the lunch room alone. She noticed a newspaper folded in half partially tucked in the couch and strolled over to read it. Sitting, she pulled out the Metro section, reading the headline *"Joseph Stacolli to Be Honored by City Council"*. Ovasta glared at the accompanying photo beneath. The caption cited Mr. Stacolli and his security guard James Williams who was standing in the background. She peered at the photo. *It...it couldn't be.* Visions of Williams flooded her mind. Piercing blue eyes, hot breath, cheap cologne. Nausea snuck in, commandeering disbelief. The room appeared to be shrinking. A tightness gripped her throat. Unable to breathe, she grabbed the paper, running down the hospital corridors to the restroom.

Once again, the moment in the alley taunted her. Mocked her. The laughter, the scorn, the comments. Even the money. *Why throw money at me? Was that a joke? Why did they say the creep didn't pay me? Who were they talking about?* Sweat coated her body. Gut-wrenching pain filled her stomach. Reaching the restroom, she entered the first stall, dry heaving. After a few minutes, the outer door to the restroom could be heard gently creaking open.

"Vee, are you in here?" whispered Riya, only partially in the bathroom. "Someone saw you racing down the hallway."

"Yes, I'm in here." Ovasta emerged out of the stall like Frankenstein's monster. Stiff. Dragging forward. Slumped shoulders. Tears surging down her cheeks.

Riya hurried towards her, wrapping her arms around Ovasta's taut body. "Oh, honey, what happened?" Riya's voice shuddering.

"He's in the paper. I can't believe he's in the paper." Ovasta's voice cracked.

"Who's in the paper?"

Ovasta held the newspaper up, pointing. Her hands shaking intensely. "That's the guy who forced the young man to rape me."

Riya took the newspaper, studying the photograph. Ovasta dashed to the faucet, turning it on, splashing cold water in her face.

Riya went over to her and patted her on the back. "Don't worry, Vee. This is good news. Now we know who he is. We can go to the police." Riya grabbed a paper towel, handing it to Ovasta. "Here. Wipe your face and take some deep breaths and try to relax."

Ovasta panted for a few seconds. "Call Vince, I want to go to the station right now."

Within twenty minutes, Ovasta, Vince, and Riya arrived at the police station. Officer Daniels met them at the front desk.

"Good afternoon. I'm glad to see you all. Please follow me. My desk is right down the hall."

Daniels led them through a maze of desks in an open area of the dank, dreary station. The air filled with chatter, ringing telephones, and the pecking of fingers pressing down on computer keyboards. The windowless brick walls made it seem like the officers themselves were being held captive.

"Have a seat, ma'am," commanded Officer Daniels as she approached her desk. She pulled out a chair whose orange cloth covering appeared soiled. Daniels continued smirking. "Don't worry, it's been sterilized. I clean around here on a regular basis. You can't afford to get careless in this day and age."

Ovasta reluctantly sat down in the chair.

Officer Daniels pointed to two other chairs for Vince and Riya located at another desk. "You guys can pull those over here. The officers who sit there are on the beat right now."

Vince picked up both chairs, placing one on each side of Ovasta.

"Thank you for meeting with us on such short notice," stated Ovasta.

"I'm glad I could. Let me get your case file." Daniels went to a tall beige metal cabinet, pulling out the second drawer. She grabbed a folder, then closed the drawer swiftly. She sat down, pushing aside a pile of papers on her cluttered desk.

"Let me see what I have here. You weren't able to give me much of a description before. You explained over the phone that you had new information?"

"I do." Ovasta handed her the Metro section of the paper. "That's him in the background." Ovasta writhed in her seat as Daniels peered at the photo.

"Had you ever met him before?"

"No. I'd never seen him before."

"I'll bring him in for questioning."

"You know where he lives?" Vince broke in.

"Practically everyone in town knows where the Stacolli family lives. The area they live in is so exclusive, you can't miss it. Maybe Mr. Williams can give us more information about the other parties as well. I'm going to get to the bottom of this. Even if he doesn't give me any other names, I've got plenty to book him on. Are you sure he took you against your will, forced you in his car, and threatened you with a gun?" Daniels grimly looked at Ovasta while pointing to Williams' picture in the paper.

"Yes. I'm absolutely sure it was him."

"You know this means you'll have to testify. It won't be easy."

"I made it this far. I can do this." Turning toward Vince, then Riya, she put her hands on both of their knees. "I have a lot of support."

"That's good to hear. Let me escort you all back to the waiting area so you can go home. I'll call you as soon as I can."

"Thanks. I look forward to hearing from you."

Officer Daniels led them back to the front of the building, shook their hands, and went back to her desk.

"That went well. Didn't it, Vee?" asked Riya unsure about Ovasta's reaction.

A faint smile brushed Ovasta's face. "I think it did. I'm feeling much better. Hopeful. I know I'll have to testify but I can do this. The odds are he won't implicate the other two men. But I'll find them. Some way, somehow," she declared with a determination in her voice.

Vince stared into Ovasta's eyes then put his arm around her shoulders. Riya joined in. All three left the police station together. Talking. Laughing. Something they hadn't done in several months.

CHAPTER
EIGHT

O vasta arrived at work early feeling quite refreshed. Nightmares had withdrawn their ugly grip from her slumber for several nights in a row. Driving past snow-covered trees now decorated with holiday lights also aided in uplifting her spirits. Entering her office, she hung up her wool coat and scarf, putting the leather gloves in the pocket. *I believe it's time to have a long talk with Vince,* she thought, sitting in her office chair, her head resting on the back. Anxiously, she slid the engagement ring up and down her finger. *You're like the elephant in the room. Nobody wants to talk about it but everybody notices.* A smile traveled to the curve of her lips as John Legend's ringtone sang through her cell phone announcing Vince's phone call.

"Good morning. How are you?" asked Ovasta, her voice sounding melodic.

"I'm good, are you at work already?" asked Vince on the other end sounding surprised.

"I sure am."

"I'll be there in a minute. How about a different flavor of coffee today?" He happily queried.

"Sure, that's fine. See you in a minute." Ovasta placed the phone on the desk, debating how to talk to him. Arriving within minutes, Vince, dressed in black dress pants, white dress shirt and a white lab coat, leaned his muscular body in the office doorway with a cup of coffee in each hand.

"Can I come in?" he questioned, sporting a sly smile.

"Since when did you start asking?"

"Just checking," he responded, playfully winking.

Vince ambled slowly into the office, avoiding coffee spillage, the brisk odor of dark-roasted mocha preceding him. She met him in front of the desk taking the cup out of his hand.

"You looked well rested today," his dancing eyes skimmed her face.

"Thank you. I'm feeling a little better every day. I've been doing a lot of thinking lately.

"What have you been thinking about?"

"Us."

Vince raised his eyebrows. "What about us?"

"Where do we go from here?"

"I want to go to the same place we were headed before. The altar. Nothing that has happened can ever change that."

"Vince, I love you but . . . I'm not sure I can love like you deserve to be loved. The assault took a part of me. I wouldn't want to cheat you by not giving you all of my heart."

"I understand. You've been through a terrible ordeal. These things take time. I'm a patient man, I'll wait."

Her tear-filled eyes caressed him. She glided her hand across his cheek. He closed his eyes, savoring the moment.

Softly grabbing her hand he pulled it around his body, placing it in the small of his back. Nestling her cheeks with both hands he gently stroked her lips with his mouth. "I'd rather live a lie with you than in truth without you." His sultry voice, like a heat-seeking missile, found her heart, piercing it like a knife.

"Can you meet me after work at my house around six? I'd like to cook dinner for you, just the two of us, then we can finish this conversation."

"Six it is." Vince paused, then took two steps backwards, eyeing Ovasta, his entire being longing for her. "I definitely need to leave. This is a public place, you know."

"I know," replied Ovasta blushing. "See you later."

"You can count on it."

Vince left the office swiftly after taking his coffee off her desk. Ovasta watched him leave, white lab coat swaying as his lengthy legs strode out. She reflected on the past couple of moments—no flashbacks, no anxiety, no uneasiness. Only warmth. Passion. She considered herself unequivocally blessed. After all, Vince was a very attractive man and on top of that, he was a doctor. Women at the hospital swooned over him. Actually, women everywhere they went did. However, he paid them absolutely no attention at all. He was an honest man who only had eyes for her. He said so on many occasions. Riya would jokingly say it, but it was true. He was her prince charming. She couldn't wait until six o'clock.

Ovasta left work early in order to prepare dinner for Vince. It had been a while since she cooked anything let alone a full course meal. Rushing in the door, she was greeted by Major who barked excitedly, happy to see her as always.

Kneeling, she hugged him and patted him on the head and then got up and hung her hat and coat in the closet by the door.

"Let's go in my room, boy. I've got to change into my *other* work clothes."

Following her, Major sat down quietly next to the bed as she put on a pair of jeans and a sweatshirt. She went to the kitchen, grabbing a bag of charcoal and some lighter fluid and matches from the cabinet nearest the back door. Vince was a steak-and-potatoes man and although it was cold, she decided to fire up the grill. Ovasta slid back the red taffeta curtain exposing the glass door which separated the patio from the dining area.

She unlocked and slid the door open, moving hurriedly as her sweatshirt was no match for the wintry air. Quickly, she threw in the coals, doused them with lighter fluid, then tossed in a match. Flames and sparks lit up the night sky like Fourth of July fireworks, the heat providing a brief respite from the chill.

Once the flames calmed, Ovasta went back into the kitchen opening the refrigerator and pulling out two top sirloin steaks which were marinating with a dry herb rub. Major, watched her and began panting and wagging his tail, perhaps hoping for a steak dinner.

"This is not for you, Major, but I did find a steak with the bone in it. You can have it after we're done." Ovasta put the steaks on the kitchen table and grabbed a can of wet dog food as well as a bag of dry food from underneath the kitchen sink, mixing them together in a bowl on the counter. She put water on the other side of the bowl, placing it on the floor. Major gobbled his food down like he hadn't eaten in weeks. Ovasta laughed as she ran her hand across the black fur on his back.

Picking up her tablet from the counter, she retrieved her playlist containing the top twenty songs of the 70s. Al Green played in the background while she finished preparing baked potatoes and vegetable kebobs with pineapples for the grill.

Dinner was finished around 5:40. Ovasta placed fine china with gold-trimmed edging on the table, complemented with wine glasses for the Argentine red wine. Beige and red floating candles in a spherical glass vase accented the table's center. After sending Vince a text asking him to use his emergency key to let himself in, she took a quick shower as she smelled of smoke. By the time she was dressed, Vince was sitting on the couch waiting for her.

"Hey, Vince, I thought I heard some noise. Were you talking to someone?"

Vince looked up smiling. "Hi, sweetie. Yes. I was talking to Major about how I was feeling today. He's a pretty good listener, you know. Never any backtalk." Vince stood with a bouquet of flowers in his hand extending them towards her.

"Oh, thank you, honey!" Ovasta exclaimed. "I'll get a vase to put them in. Now come take a seat at the dinner table."

"Yes, ma'am, but can I at least get a hug and a kiss first?"

"I swear, you men have a one-track mind," smirked Ovasta, shaking her head. Vince moved closer to her. He clutched her, giving a light squeeze and a peck on the lips. "I actually have a two-track mind because I definitely want to eat." Vince went into the dining room.

Ovasta went to the kitchen with the flowers and put them in a vase which was on top of her refrigerator. After placing them inside then adding water, she sat them on the kitchen table and took the food out of the warmer.

"Do you need any help?" Vince asked from the other room.

"Why don't you open the wine and pour it into the glasses."

"Okay. Let me know if you need anything else."

Ovasta placed the food on a large tray and brought it into the dining room. Vince took the tray from her and placed it on the table.

"You should have let me get this while you poured the wine."

Ovasta gave him a retreating smile.

He uncovered the silver platter, observing the food. "This looks fantastic. Wow!" He hesitated. "You grilled the steak!" Vince's widened eyes appeared pleased. Pulling out the chair for her, he motioned for her to sit down. "The least I can do is serve you." After putting the cloth napkin from the place setting on her lap, he set a plate of food in front of her and sat beside her. "Where's your sidekick?" he teased.

"I spoke to Riya earlier today. She has another date with Orlando."

Vince picked up a knife and fork then began cutting his steak into pieces. "So, they're hitting it off pretty well, I assume."

"It seems that way. Hopefully, the four of us will be going out soon."

"I'm so glad to hear that you're still saying *us*." Vince put his fork down, eyeing her intently.

Ovasta expelled a small sigh. "So much for talking after the meal is over."

"I thought that was why we were having the meal, so we could talk." His quick, sharp response caused a few beads of sweat to form on her hairline.

She sliced her potato width wise. "I wanted to eat first."

"We can wait until after dinner if you'd like. I've waited this long. What's another few minutes?" Vince picked his fork back up, jabbing it into a piece of steak, then shoved the steak in his mouth chewing vigorously.

"Vince, you are the most wonderful man I could ever have hoped for. If it weren't for you and Riya, I don't believe I'd be doing as well as I am. Every once in a while I have flashbacks. Sometimes it's still a struggle to get out of bed. It is not often but it happens. I want to marry you. I don't want to lose you. But how are you going to handle the days when I may be afraid for you to touch me?"

"Losing me was never an option. We'll have to take things one day at a time. However, if we never take the leap of faith, it will never happen. Part of overcoming the fear is facing it. Also, you are getting professional help on each step of your journey. We can go to counseling together if you want. I'm open to anything." Vince extended his hand towards her. She grabbed it, holding on tightly. His large hand overshadowed hers.

Overwhelmed, Ovasta began to cry. Before she knew it she felt Vince's warm embrace. He picked up a napkin and wiped her face.

"Thank you for loving me," she sobbed.

He put his forehead on hers. "You're so very welcome."

Ovasta gathered her composure. "I liked the idea of getting counseling together. How about pre-marital counseling? I'm sure Mrs. Lions, could recommend someone," she said softly.

"Then counseling it is. Does that mean we're going to pick a date?"

"Yes, before the night is over," she whispered as she leaned forward and kissed him.

"Alright, let's do this." A broad grin covered Vince's face. He got up and sat back at the table. "How about we finish our meal and then start planning our lives together."

The next day, Ovasta and Riya met at a diner near the hospital for lunch. Riya arrived first sitting in their favorite spot—the back booth nearest the window. Although nearly noon, most people visited Dina's Diner for its magnificent breakfast dishes served all day long. Riya and Ovasta ate there at least once a month, having tried every breakfast food on the menu.

As Ovasta arrived in the parking lot and got out of her car, she could see Riya staring out the window. Riya saw her and waved excitedly like a kid in a candy store. Ovasta rushed inside not only to meet her but to escape the blustery winds. Shortly, she joined Riya, sliding across the red vinyl seat, picking up the menu which was already placed atop a paper placemat on the oval wooden table. She pulled off her hat, coat, and gloves, laying them on the empty space beside her. They sat across from each other smiling.

"Hi, Vee, you look awfully happy today. You're almost glowing."

"Hey, Riya. I'm not glowing. I think my face is just cold." Ovasta chattered her teeth and shook her body in a shivering motion, chuckling.

"You sound like Vince, always the comedian. So how is your Prince Charming anyway? I haven't seen him today." Riya swiftly moved her eyebrows in an upward and downward motion like Groucho Marx.

"Vince is great. We had a long heartfelt conversation last night and have decided to move forward with the wedding."

"Vee, I couldn't be happier for you but are you sure you're ready for this?"

"I've been going to both individual and group therapy for what feels like a lifetime and I'm as ready as I'll ever be. It's time to move forward. We've picked a date. March fifteenth."

"What!" exclaimed Riya, eyes bulging, voice squealing, jaw dropping. "That's only a couple of months away!"

"I know. But you know how much I love Vince and have always wanted to marry him. It's now or never. I can't afford to let love pass me by."

Riya leaned forward, giving a pensive look. "Again, I'm so happy for you. And I care for you and Vince. But I do have some concerns. It seems so . . . rushed, especially after what you've been through. Sometimes the wounds on the inside are harder to heal."

"Don't worry. It was my idea. I'm much better and I want this more than ever. With good planning, it can be done. Plus Vince and I decided to get premarital counseling and he'll accompany me to my individual therapy if needed." Ovasta reached across the table, putting her hand on top of Riya's.

"I trust your judgment, Vee. Always have."

"Thanks. You know I feel the same way about you. Don't worry, things are going to work out fine. With that being said, today, lunch is on me." Ovasta turned sideways, flagging the waitress to the table, who scuttled over to them as if she had been awaiting her cue. The overhead fluorescent lights seem to follow her tall, slender frame.

"Hi, my name is Donna. I'll be serving you today."

"We're going to have omelets with everything in them, pancakes, hash browns, and orange juice," Ovasta blurted out with glee.

"Sounds good to me," agreed Riya, laughing.

"Thanks, ladies. I'll be back with your juices in a few

minutes." Donna grinned, revealing a chipped front tooth on the right side of her mouth. Her long narrow hands took the menus from off the table putting them in the large pocket of her plaid blue-and-white apron which was wrapped tightly around her thin waistline. Swiftly, she left the table, her long brown ponytail trailing behind her.

As soon as the waitress turned away, Riya started talking. "Alright, so what's the plan?" Riya leaned her body partially across the table. "Are we going shopping again like we did right before the Director's Ball?" she continued.

"Yeah, that's the plan and I have to call Vince's cousin to make sure she's available to be in the wedding party on the fifteenth."

"Where are you having the ceremony?"

"We are still going with the cathedral near the hospital. The same place we were talking about having it before. Vince is supposed to be taking care of that. He'll let me know either way if we can get that date. They also have a hall there which can be rented out for the reception."

"I've been there before. That hall is beautiful," gushed Riya.

"Hopefully, I can still use Renee's Catering Company as well. I had spoken to them previously before all this happened. We can do this. It will all work out in the end."

"I agree."

Out of the corner of her eye, Ovasta saw the waitress bringing their food. "Man, that looks good. I haven't had omelets in a long time."

"Me either. Let's eat."

After eating and making more wedding plans, Ovasta and Riya left the diner. Riya got in her car which was parked next to the building. Ovasta was parked in the row behind her.

"See you later," said Ovasta giving Riya an air kiss, as Riya got in her car.

"Okay." Riya air kissed back.

Ovasta's cell phone rang as she was opening her car door. She jumped in quickly as a gust of wind pushed the door outward almost hitting the car beside it.

"Hello," she answered after slamming the door shut and turning the key in the ignition.

"Hello, this is Officer Daniels calling. Is this Miss Kaiser?"

"Yes, it is. You have news about my case?" There was silence on the other end of the phone. Ovasta got worried. "Officer Daniels, are you still there?"

"Yes. I have some bad news, ma'am," replied Daniels, her voice monotonous.

Ovasta squinted. "Bad news? How could there possibly be bad news?"

"Your lead was a dead end. At the advice of my sergeant, I'm going to close your case."

"A dead end. Are you kidding me? What does that mean? Please explain that to me. Did you even interview Mr. Williams?" Ovasta's voice became elevated.

"No, ma'am. But we did speak to his attorney. Basically, it's your word against his. There is absolutely no evidence to back your claims."

Pain shot throughout Ovasta's body, causing victimization to return. "You spoke to his attorney. What innocent man needs an attorney? Did you speak to anyone else? Perhaps his boss or maybe a neighbor. Did you even try to find the other men he was working with? Or, what about the young man? Who is he? Did you look for him at all? It doesn't seem as if any real effort is being made to solve this case. I don't want to talk to you anymore. Give me your sergeant's phone number. I'm going to give him a call. If he doesn't answer my questions, then I'll call the news media. Somebody is going to bring that man to justice."

"I can hear you're upset. I'm so very sorry. These cases are hard to prove and there is no physical evidence linking Williams to you. The only evidence we have is from the rape kit which links the assault to the young man whom you stated was also a victim. I'm not sure it will help but I'll give you Sergeant Rider's number. Maybe he can explain things a little better. I hate to say this but the Stacolli family is very powerful and they've done a lot for this community. The news article you brought to the precinct only highlights some of Mr. Stacolli's contributions. That's why he's being honored next week. You'll be hard pressed to find someone who'll go against him no matter who you question. Even still, we have to prove beyond a reasonable doubt that Williams is responsible. You said yourself that he acted as if you knew what was going on. If he did think you were someone else, then his intent was not to harm you."

Ovasta's mounting rage was propelled by Officer Daniels' matter-of-fact attitude. "Why are you talking about Mr. Stacolli? He wasn't even there. I'm talking about Williams. I tried to tell him he had the wrong person. More than once. He wouldn't let me speak. If his intent was not to harm me then why did he pull his gun out? *Tell me why!* Williams should be punished for what he did. Not only to me, but to the young man also." Tears flowed down her face as she placed her head down on the steering wheel in disbelief. Suddenly, her mind went back to the night in the limo with Williams. Gradually lifting her head from the steering wheel, her rapid eye movement retrieved the painful memory. "Officer, I remember Williams said someone was on the take in the police department. That's probably why the case is being dropped," she said, a tiny glimmer of hope in her voice.

"Did you get a name?" Daniels asked disdainfully.

"No." Ovasta's response was barely audible. It seemed the whole world was crashing down on her.

"I'm sorry I can't be of more assistance. If you have a pen, I'll give you Sergeant Rider's direct phone number."

"Hold on for a moment."

Ovasta reached for the black-and-tan Dooney and Bourke purse from the passenger's seat. The zipper felt like lead in her trembling hands. Struggling, she managed to unzip the top and retrieve a ballpoint pen. Nervously rummaging through her purse, she found a grocery store receipt to write on. After obtaining the phone number from Officer Daniels, she abruptly hung up the phone. Frantically, she dialed Sergeant Rider.

"Sergeant Rider speaking."

The harsh gritty voice took Ovasta aback. "Hello, sir, my name is Ovasta Kaiser. Officer Daniels was working on my case and—"

"I know why you're calling. I told Daniels to close the case due to lack of evidence. Mr. Williams has an alibi. He was nowhere near that hotel on the night of the incident." Rider's boorish attitude infuriated Ovasta.

"That's an absolute lie! He was there! Never mind you or Daniels. I'm going to call the news media. Everyone needs to know that the police department makes no effort to solve rape cases. I identified the perpetrator and brought his name and picture to you. Basically, I handed you the man on a silver platter. Now it's time for you to do your job." Her voice grew deeper as she spoke each word.

Rider sounded exasperated by her tone. "Ms. Kaiser, the case is closed. If you want to call the new media, you are more than welcome to do so. However, I am no longer willing to discuss this case with you. Have a good day." Rider hung up the phone not waiting for a response.

The dead silence of the phone aggravated her even more. Ovasta angrily threw her cell on the passenger's seat. One vein in the middle of her forehead expanded in concert with her flaring nostrils. She slammed her hand on the steering wheel causing the horn to sound. *Breathe. Breathe. In through the nose and out through the mouth.*

She sat in her car in the diner parking lot. Alone. Watching the snowflakes fall on the windshield of her soul. Embittered. Embattled. *I can't let him get away with this.*

He has got to pay. Ovasta picked her phone back up and searched for the number to city hall.

"Hello, my name is Ovasta Kaiser. I'd like to know how I can get my name on the guest list for Mr. Stacolli's celebration luncheon."

NINE

I t was one of the coldest days in mid-December ever recorded. One could see the glacier-like accumulations across rooftops for miles. At the gated community where the Stacolli's lived, maintenance crews worked hard to ensure there was no ice on the walkways as they prepared to leave their home to attend Joseph's celebration luncheon. Joseph had fallen the previous year, breaking the tibia and the fibula bones in his right ankle.

"Maria, would you check outside to see if the ice has been cleared away?" asked Stella as she entered the vestibule.

Maria opened the custom-made metal front door, surveying the frozen landscape, the wind blowing her long salt-and-pepper hair. "I think they're done, ma'am," she replied said to Stella after closing the door.

"Thank you for checking. We don't want any more accidents. As you're well aware Joseph has fallen before. I definitely don't want that to happen again. He's still got a pin in his ankle from the surgery. We get stopped by TSA every time we go to the airport."

"Yes, ma'am." Maria nodded her head giving Stella a

gander. "You look beautiful today. The purple dress complements your hair and eyes."

Stella smiled at her. "Why thank you, Maria. What a nice thing to say. It's something I picked up when Joseph and I went to New York this summer. He said it reminded him of one of the cocktail dresses Nancy Reagan wore when she was First Lady." Stella's eyes twinkled while recalling the moment.

"She looks regal, doesn't she, Maria?" asked Joseph, strolling into the vestibule.

"Yes, sir, I was just complimenting her, and congratulations to you, Mr. Stacolli. I'm glad that someone recognizes all your contributions to this city. Today's luncheon is a real honor."

"Thanks, Maria. I appreciate the sentiment. Actually, I really think you should be coming. You're more like family than hired help. You've seen us through thick and thin. You are both loyal and trustworthy. We couldn't ask for better."

Maria's chubby cheeks turned beet red. "I'm humbled, sir. It's been a joy being here. I can't imagine working anywhere else." she replied.

"I know we normally only allow you to leave at noon on Christmas Eve and get Christmas Day off. But this year, I want you to take six or seven days off this month with pay. It's holiday time. Spend it with your family. Let us know as soon as possible which days you plan to be off. Also, we'll be sure to double your Christmas bonus so you can spend it on those beautiful grandchildren of yours."

Maria placed both hands over her dropped jaw. She

blinked her eyes several times in a row in hopes of averting the flow of tears from her eyes. "Thank you so much, Mr. Stacolli. I appreciate it more than you'll ever know."

Stella moved closer to her and patted her on the back. "Why don't you finish up what you were doing and go home. We're going out to enjoy ourselves and we want you to do the same," whispered Stella in her ear.

"Thank you! Your limo should be here any moment. Thanks, again." Maria scurried away.

Joseph and Stella chuckled as they watched her leave. "She's running like a bird freed from its cage," joked Joseph.

"I know. Maybe she thinks we'll change our minds. In the future, we'll have to stop making her stay here so late. For the most part, it's only the two of us. I think we can manage without having her here all the time. But enough about Maria. Did I tell you how handsome you are in your black tailored suit and striped gray-and-black tie?" Stella asked, playfully winking at her husband.

"I don't believe you have," responded Joseph, smirking.

Stella glided towards Joseph with the grace and poise of Queen Elizabeth and threw her arms around his neck. After giving him a peck on the lips, she laid her head on his chest.

"You're the most handsome man I know. I'd do anything for you . . . anything for *us*. You know that, right?" Stella murmured in a sultry voice. A sideways grin radiating with perniciousness donned her face.

"Yeah, I know, peaches. I know." Joseph squeezed Stella tightly, his chest pulsating.

For Stella, listening to Joseph's heartbeat was like hearing ocean waves as they ebb and flow across the distant seashore. She wished the moment could last forever but was grateful it had lasted a lifetime.

"You know we have to get going, honey?" Joseph's voice reverberated in her ear.

"I know. But being near you makes me happy." Stella lifted her head, staring into his eyes. "I'm so proud of you. I'm so proud to be Mrs. Joseph Stacolli."

"Stella, with those words you got all of my heart. I'll never yearn for another. I love you, too, peaches. Marrying you was the best thing I've ever done." Joseph stopped for a moment, beholding his wife of almost fifty years, marveling that she was still so full of life and energy. "Let me get your coat. The driver should be outside waiting."

He got her full-length fox fur coat out of the closet near the front door, helping her to put it on and grabbed his wool topcoat and hat. When he opened the door, he was greeted by Stokes who helped both of them down the stairs and into the car.

Due to someone's last-minute cancelation, Ovasta was able to obtain a ticket to Stacolli's celebration luncheon at the City Council Club. Arriving around 10:45 a.m., she darted into the club's restroom, going into the last of five stalls. There she removed her wool coat, classic white top, and pin-striped calf-length skirt to reveal a formfitting short-sleeve V-necked black dress which barely reached her knees and had sequins from the waist up. She pulled a red wig and John Lennon-like round glasses out of her large Coach bag, stuffed her clothes inside, and sprinted from the stall to the large square-shaped mirror. Fixing her wig, ensuring none of her black hair was showing, and resting the glasses on her nose, she strutted out of the restroom.

The hostess checked her reservation and Ovasta surveyed the room prior to walking in. She noticed several people whom she feared would recognize her. Holding her head down, she weaved through the crowd towards the bar which was in the back of the room near the kitchen, almost bumping into Stacolli. He was taking pictures with the mayor in front of the podium decorated with poinsettias and holiday lights. Once at the bar, she exhaled a sigh of relief.

"I'm going to the restroom, then to the limo for a smoke. I should be back in about ten minutes."

Ovasta's ears tingled, recognizing the voice. One of the three voices which haunted her for months. *Stokes.* Standing within three feet of her. Talking to another gentleman whom she did not recognize. The sight of him produced a tightness in her throat, making it a struggle to breathe. For a moment she stood there, somewhat paralyzed by his presence. Her mind raced. Her heart pounded. Beads of sweat formed on her forehead. After a few seconds, she managed to compose herself and contemplate what her next step would be. Yesterday, things had played out so much easier in her mind. But this was reality. She underestimated how much seeing him would affect her and wondered what to do next. *I'll try the direct approach. I have no time for games.*

Ovasta closed her eyes for a moment and gathered her thoughts. "I'd like to get two Sprites, please," she said, turning to the bartender.

The bartender poured the drinks and placed them in front of her. The moment he turned away, she took a glass bottle out of her bag and with her jittery hand, poured the contents into one of the drinks. She put her coat on, tossed her purse strap across her shoulder, and picked up both glasses, deliberately sidling up to Stokes with the drinks in front of her.

"Hi, remember me?" she whispered breathily. Stokes glared at her with no recognition in his eyes.

"You remember, from the alley about three months ago. *He* sent me back as an apology for my behavior. I wasn't my best that day. And you were right, he hadn't paid me." Ovasta leaned towards Stokes' face giving him a sly look. "He gave me double this time to make up for it. For you . . . and Williams," she continued. Ovasta winked her right eye at Stokes and offered him a Sprite.

"Oh, I remember you now. The red hair and glasses kind of threw me off. By the way, you look better with dark hair." Stokes appeared amused. He grabbed the Sprite and gulped it down quickly, then grimaced at the glass. "I was hoping for something a little stronger."

"You really shouldn't drink and drive," she replied, a nervous giggle in her voice. He stared at her with his small brown eyes, breathing heavily. She felt like he was groping her. Queasiness engulfed her body like heat in a dry desert. To end the moment, she reached for his glass, careful not to touch his hand. "Let me get that for you."

He handed her the glass, giving her a creepy smile with his large, tar-stained teeth. "Just so you know, Williams isn't here today. Boss has him on another assignment. But you can meet me in about ten minutes at the limo. Stokes pointed towards the back of the room. Go out that door and through the rear of the hotel. It's on the north side of the building." Stokes swayed into the restroom like a hunter going to retrieve his kill.

After placing the drinks down on a nearby table, Ovasta pulled her hair to the front in order to hide her face while leaving the luncheon. Before exiting the building, she rushed back to the restroom splashing water on her face several times to help subside the pricking feeling on her skin. *Hopefully, this will be the end of it. I'm not going to get Williams but at least I'll get one of them. Then I can put this behind me and get on with my life.* She put the glasses back on her face after patting it dry with a paper towel purposely never having looked at her reflection in the mirror above the sink. "Let's get this over with," she whispered to herself while proceeding out of the restroom.

When she arrived at the back of the building she was taken aback at the sight of the limo. Imagines of Williams forcing her inside began to flood her mind. She wanted to turn around and go back inside. But it was too late. Stokes was already there, standing next to the limo, cigarette in his mouth. Leering. Although not as muscular as Williams, his six-foot body appeared extremely fit in his tailored black suit.

"I thought you stood me up. Maybe taking the money and running away with it, seeing as how you've already been paid," he snarled after blowing smoke out of his mouth.

"No, I went to the restroom to freshen up. I wouldn't have missed this for the world. I would never stand anyone up." A forced smile traversed her lips.

"Why are you standing so far away?" complained Stokes noticing the distance between them.

"Smoke really bothers my breathing. I'll wait until you are finished. No need to rush."

Stokes turned his lip up, almost growling. "Just what I need, an asthmatic hooker." He reached in his pocket, hit the key fob, unlocked the limo doors, and opened the back door. "Get in. It's very cold out here and your face is turning red."

Ovasta knew her face being red was due to more than the cold weather. Panic had set in. Wondering why the drug hadn't taken effect yet. She would have thought he'd have passed out by now. Yet there he was. Standing upright. Maybe she had not poured enough solution in his drink. It was too late to second guess herself. Gradually, she walked over to the limo and slid across the back seat. A sharp pain tore through her body when she closed the limo door. She paused. Another flashback. Before she had been forced inside. This time it was her own doing. Her thoughts overwhelmed her. *God help me. Am I really going to have to go through with this?*

"Take your coat and dress off. I'll be with you in a minute. I got a phone call to make." Stokes turned away, pulling his cell phone out of his pocket. However, Ovasta could still hear him talking.

"Hey, can you give me another twenty minutes? I got some serious business to take care of," he said to the other voice on the phone. He opened the door; sneering down at her. "Why are you still dressed? You even have on gloves." At first, Stokes frowned, but it quickly turned into a mischievous smile. "Never mind, I'll help you with your clothes. It will be much more fun that way."

Stokes slithered on top of her, his cold clammy hands pulling her dress up as he went. He grabbed her face with one hand. With the other, he unbuckled his pants. Putting his mouth on hers, he kissed her, his grip too strong for her to turn away. In an instant, his head fell over to one side. His speech slurred.

"What's going on? I feel weak." His head rolled over to the side of her cheek. As he breathed heavily, the smell of nicotine filled the air. Out of the corner of her eye, she could see him blinking, slowly, purposefully. His brown eyes pierced hers. "Where am I and who are you?"

"You're in Mr. Stacolli's limo. Why don't you try to get out and I'll get you a glass of water or something. Maybe even call for help."

Stokes didn't respond immediately. Moving sluggishly he partially slid down her body. Stopping, he rested his head on her stomach, his limp body felt like lead. "Can't . . . move," he stuttered.

"Try again," cried Ovasta as she was struggling to inhale, fearing she wouldn't be able to get from underneath him. He lifted up a little more. Pushing, straining, grunting, sweating, Ovasta managed to push him to one side. Inch by inch, she maneuvered her body out of the limo.

Outside, she inhaled a large pocket of frigid air, chilling her lungs, causing her to wheeze. Glancing down at Stokes, she noticed that his long brawny legs hung outside the limo, exposing his argyle socks and Stacy Adams shoes which pointed towards the ground. His body was slightly contorted as the back of his head leaned against the back of the front seat. He managed to lift himself up, then pushed backwards on his elbows. Finally, his knees hit the ground. The impact made him groan.

Snatching the back of his collar with all her might, Ovasta dragged him down on the dirt. There he lay face up motionless, mouth agape, eyes wide open. Angrily she scanned him, glove-clad fists clenched, pushing large amounts of air out of her lungs while circling his fit physique like an animal preparing to attack its prey.

"You and your friends think you can do anything and get away with it. You almost ruined my life. *Our* lives. There were times when I could hardly bear for Vince to look at me, let alone touch me." Ovasta spoke through gritted teeth, tears traveling down her cheek, panting. The breath from her nostrils met the icy air, giving the appearance of puffs of smoke.

Lifting her right leg, she swung her black stiletto into his midsection. Adrenaline flowed through her being, sweat poured down her face, anger filled her heart.

"That was for all my sleepless nights." She swung a second time, the impact so hard, pain shot from her foot to her ankle crawling up her leg. Stokes coughed. Blood filled his mouth.

"That was for Vince." Ovasta glanced around the back of the building in search for something else to attack Stokes with. She saw a tailpipe from a car lying on the ground near the front of the limo. Limping, she hobbled over, picked it up, and tottered back to Stokes. Holding the tailpipe like a baseball bat, trembling from the cold, she shook her head back and forth. Staring at his body lying helplessly on the ground. Ovasta began to shout, veins popping out of her neck. "Scum! You're not worth it! You're not worth going to jail for! You're not worth losing my freedom!"

"Hey! What are you doing?" yelled a voice from the back entrance. Startled, Ovasta dropped the pipe on the ground, shivering, afraid to look up. "It is you," said the voice in amazement, moving closer. The voice was familiar, another from her nightmares. She gave him a stare square in the face. It *was* him. The young man whom they forced to assault her. Standing there. Squinted eyes, eyebrows knit. Full-length gray wool coat, Kangol hat, black dress pants and those black patent leather shoes. The ones from the alley. The ones which trampled through her dreams.

"Is he *dead*?" he questioned as he glared down at Stokes, whose body was between them.

"No, only wounded. I decided he wasn't worth going to jail for. Nobody is. He already tried to take a piece of my life. I can't give him the rest."

"How did you get him down on the ground?"

Ovasta paused wondering if she should respond to his question. Knowing if she did there could be serious consequences. Reluctantly, she responded. "I put a little something in his drink. When he wakes up, he won't remember a thing unless you tell him." Momentarily, Ovasta's heart stopped beating.

"Are you sure he won't remember?" He questioned, smiling.

Ovasta heard mischief in the young man's tone. "Yes. I work in a hospital and have seen many patients who've been under the influence of this drug. Memory loss is one of the side effects."

Strolling around Stokes and closer to Ovasta, he gave her an impish smile, his eyes twinkling with delight. Ovasta gave him a sideways glare, not understanding his mood.

Without warning, he stomped his foot into Stokes' groin area. "Prick, now who's not a man? I hope you never reproduce another child." He started shuffling his feet, moving his arms and fists and bobbing his head from side to side like Muhammad Ali right before the Thrilla in Manila.

"Oh, my God, please, you've got to stop," shrieked Ovasta. Her knees started to buckle, her body exploding with fear.

"Ma'am, you really don't understand. Williams, Stokes, and Jones continue to harass me when my parents and grandparents are not around. Calling me names like 'gay boy' and 'faggot.' I'm sick of it!" His head started jerking to the right side, almost like a nervous twitch, tears rushing down his cheeks.

"My name is Ovasta, what's yours?" She spoke in a calm soothing manner in hopes of diffusing the young man's rage.

"I'm Joseph Stacolli's grandson. Ralph Stacolli Jr. but you can call me Junnie."

"Junnie, he's not worth it. Stop and think about it. This is something you will have to live with the rest of your life. That's why I changed my mind. Why I decided not to hit him with the pole."

They stopped and stared at each other. Ovasta hoped the eyes he avoided in the alley would now comfort him. He turned away from her and stared at Stokes' body. A few moments later, his cell phone rang. He pulled it out of his pocket and read the caller-ID. "It's my dad. You'd better leave right now." He put the phone to his ear. Ovasta could hear the voice on the other line ask where he was and tell him that they were worried about him.

"Dad, I'm fine. Just stepped outside for a moment. I'll be in in a second." Junnie hung up the phone. He peered at Ovasta leaning to one side trying to hold her right leg off the ground while wiping her running nose with a piece of tissue from her pocket. "Your ankle is swollen. What happened?"

"I injured it kicking him. In trying to hurt someone else, I hurt myself in the process." Ovasta hesitated, glancing down at Stokes. "You should call an ambulance. Otherwise, he'll probably freeze to death out here," she continued.

Junnie nodded his head with a grin on his face. Ovasta gave him a wave as she hobbled away, dropping the tissue out of her hand. Noticing it hit the ground, she started to kneel and pick it up.

"Don't worry. I'll get it for you. You really need to go. Hurry." Junnie moved his hand back and forth as if he were shooing away a pet.

"Thanks. It's important that you call an ambulance immediately," replied Ovasta as she moved away from him as fast as her injured leg could take her.

"Sure thing, ma'am," replied Junnie while he watched her trail off in the distance. Glancing at Stokes' motionless body, Junnie sneered then kicked him once again in his groin area. A sinister grin covered his face as Stokes made an almost noiseless groan like he was gasping for air. Junnie pulled a red napkin out of his pocket wrapping up Ovasta's tissue with it and placed it in his pocket.

"Of course, I'll pick it up. I wouldn't want your DNA at a crime scene."

TEN

The hospital was filled with the merriment of Christmas. Volunteers from many organizations came to pass out gifts to the youngest patients. Carolers, dressed in red and white, went from room to room giving the gift of song, hoping to uplift spirits. As Ovasta ambled to her office, five children, who all appeared to be under the age of ten, began to sing. Their melodic voices echoed through the hospital corridors as "Let there be peace on earth and let it begin with me" flowed from their mouths. Ovasta pondered the words. One thing she'd learned while taking social work classes was to "do no harm." She didn't kill Stokes but felt a surge of guilt for even harming him. Drugging him. It went against everything she stood for. Everything she believed in. It was more than unethical. It was illegal. She had to right her wrongs and amend her ways. Ovasta decided to go for penance and confession right after work as there was a parish, Holy Church of the Cross, within walking distance of the hospital.

Prior to leaving, Vince and Riya came to see how she was doing. Both seemed a bit on edge but never really explained what was going on. Riya left to go on another date with Orlando and Vince went home after his last surgery. It was 7 o'clock when Ovasta left the hospital. She drove to the parish, entering its large red doors quickly and quietly.

Although close to her job, she had never attended this particular church. It was majestic. The large stone edifice was built Romanesque style—groin vaults, round arches, and beautiful stained-glass windows. She saw the confessional on the right side of the wall but noticed a red-lit cross over the door signaling it was in use. She stepped as far away from it as possible, lighting a votive candle and saying a short prayer. A sixty-something-year-old woman left the confessional weeping. Hastily, Ovasta went inside kneeling down in front of the curtain. She genuflected then put her palms together, placing her thumbs together at the edge of her bottom lip. She whispered nervously, rocking back and forth on her knees.

"Bless me, Father, for I have sinned. I haven't been to confession in over ten years. I'm not sure where to begin."

"What bothers you the most, miss?" inquired the priest with much compassion. Ovasta began to weep. "I was sexually assaulted. I told the police who the perpetrator was. Even gave them his picture and they did nothing. Absolutely nothing. Today, I sought my own vengeance. I found him, drugged him, and then kicked him while he was down. I wanted to kill him, but thankfully I couldn't. He'll be fine and won't remember a thing. I've made sure of that. But I feel ashamed. *Guilty.* Things shouldn't have gone that far. I was so bitter and angry about the police dismissing my case . . . dismissing *me* that I completely lost control of myself. I was absolutely enraged. I've never felt like this before. Even now a part of me is still in turmoil. I'm wondering if I'll ever be myself again? Will I ever come to my senses?" Ovasta's whole body ached from the inside out. Sweat gushed down her face, intermingling with her tears.

"You came to your senses when you came to God. Remember, for God so *loved* the world that He gave the life of His only son. He loves you. He has not forgotten you. Others may dismiss, He never will. But please understand that vengeance is God's job, He will repay. When you try to do it yourself, something always goes wrong. Ask God to help you let go of the anger. Let go of the bitterness in your heart. It only eats you up like a cancerous tumor spreading throughout the body. Let God be the radiation in your life that kills the cancer and restores your soul. I absolve you of your sins in the name of the Father, the Son, and the Holy Spirit. Now go in peace and love. Make an act of contrition and vow to come to church, return to the Lord. You've been gone too long."

"I will. Thanks be to God."

Ovasta left the confessional with a feeling of hope knowing God absolved her sins. After wrapping a scarf around her head and neck, she exited the large red doors determined to live life free from anger and bitterness.

The drive home was filled with anticipation of a wedding as well as moving forward with Board of Director's duties as a weight had been lifted off of her. She arrived home around 8:30 looking forward to a relaxing evening on the couch curled up with a good book and of course, Major.

The next morning Ovasta entered the hospital in a location further away from her office, jogging down the hall swiftly in her black boots, hoping it would make up for missing a week's worth of morning jogs.

"Hey, Ovasta, how are you doing?" It was Phillip's voice behind her as she was arriving at her office.

"Actually, I'm feeling pretty good. How about you?" she replied, never turning around. Phillip caught up to her as she was removing her coat.

"Let me get that for you," he said, gently taking it out of her hands.

"Why thanks. That's so generous of you."

"No problem," he replied flatly.

"Is everything okay?" she asked, noting sorrow in his voice.

Phillip hung up her coat then pulled the chair out for her. After she sat down, he sat in one of the wingback chairs, sighing. "I've had better days. But I wanted to talk to you. We never did have the discussion about what happened that night." He squinted at her, making the bags under his eyes more pronounced. "I believe I owe you an apology. I wish I could have been there for you. I *should* have been there for you." Phillip put his glasses on Ovasta's desk, wiping his watering eyes.

"Are you crying?" questioned Ovasta, in surprised. A deep sadness in her voice.

"Sort of. But not only because of the night of the Director's Ball. Someone very close to me died recently."

"I'm sorry to hear that. Is it someone I know?"

"No, I don't believe you do." His voice sounded weak. Phillip picked up his glasses, putting them back on around his black-and-gray temples.

"I'm glad you came to talk to me but there's no need. I'm doing well. Things seem to be looking up. I don't want to have the conversation because that chapter in my life is closed. There is no point in rehearsing the past. It's counterproductive." Ovasta appeared calm, peaceful.

Phillip's eyes widened with astonishment. "I'm amazed by your resilience. I thought it might be still bothering you. I thought you needed to talk. For once, I'm glad I'm wrong." Phillip tilted his head to one side with pursed lips as if contemplating what to say next. "Hey, I'm having a New Year's Eve party. I'd like you to come. We can start the New Year off right. You were right when you said there is no point in rehearsing the past or even holding on to it I might add." He paused for a moment. "Of course you know the invitation extends to Vince. He is always welcome, as well as Riya."

Ovasta struggled to keep her mouth from dropping, amazed at Phillip's invitation.

"To my knowledge, Vince has no plans. I'm not sure about Riya. She's been very busy lately. I'll ask them both and let you know."

Phillip stood up, adjusting his suit jacket, then tie.

"Please let me know by Christmas Eve. I'll wait for your response. I hope we can start anew. Get back to where we were before life changed or rather I changed."

Ovasta wasn't sure what to say. She was excited about the possibility of getting her friend back. She'd missed how close they were.

"Have a great day, Ovasta."

"You, too, Phillip."

It must be a full moon, thought Ovasta as Phillip left her office. She picked up her cell phone and texted Vince, letting him know about Phillip's invitation. Currently, he was in surgery and would be unavailable for the next several hours. She knew he'd get back to her as soon as he could.

Cheerfully, Riya sauntered into the office. "Good morning, Vee, you're here bright and early. Was that Phillip I saw coming out of here?" She plopped down in the chair in front of Ovasta's desk just as she had done for the past several years.

"Yes, and he invited all three of us to a New Year's Eve gathering at his place."

"What?" Riya's opened mouth revealed several fillings in the back teeth on her lower jaw.

"I was surprised, too. But I think we should go. What harm could it do?"

Riya shrugged her shoulders. "I don't know. I still don't trust the guy. He's got beady eyes and a sloping forehead."

"Beady eyes, sloping forehead, really," Ovasta smirked, shaking her head from side to side.

"Really." Riya slid down further into the chair, her head

resting on the back. "If *you* think he's better, then okay. Just know that he still makes me uneasy. If I have to go, I'd like to bring a plus one if I could."

"You mean Orlando?"

"Yes, things are working out pretty well for us. I'm glad I listened to my grandmother when she encouraged me to date him," replied Riya, her face radiating with joy.

"You know I couldn't be any happier. Now, let's go to the cafeteria and get some coffee. I need my morning pick-me-up and I haven't been to the store lately to buy any instant coffee."

"Okay, I've got to be going soon anyway. My break is about over."

"Since when have you ever cared about that?"

Riya rolled her eyes, then chuckled. "I see you have jokes this morning. Come on, let's go."

ELEVEN

The holidays departed, ushering in a mid-January chill which blanketed the nation. Snow covered the grass like a layer of confectioners' sugar on freshly-baked pastry. Vince and Ovasta recently had returned home after Vince's mother's unexpected illness led them to drive to Trenton, New Jersey. Shortly after celebrating Christmas at home.

Ovasta lay on the couch next to Vince, her head in his lap. "Vince, I was so glad to see your mother up and about right before we came home."

He stroked the side of her face and hair with his hand. "Me, too. Fortunately, they discovered the blockage in time. I saw her charts; she'll make a full recovery. I'm thankful both of us could take time off work so we could stay with her and my dad for the past three weeks. It was nice to be able to celebrate the New Year with them."

"You mean as opposed to going to Phillip's party."

"Exactly. I only agreed to go because you insisted." Vince tightly closed his eyes, taking a breather. "I have the worst headache ever," he moaned, placing his hand on his forehead.

Ovasta rose up from Vince's lap, put her arm around his shoulders, and began kneading the nape of his neck. "You've been through a lot and have done a lot of driving these past few weeks. Let me get you some acetaminophen, then you can get in my bed and rest. I'll turn your phone off so no one bothers you."

"Don't bother, I have to get up anyway to go to the bedroom. It doesn't make sense for both of us to move." Vince gave her a peck on the lips. "I'm so glad you came with me. What would I do without you?"

"I hope you'll never find out. Now go to bed and get some rest," stated Ovasta smiling.

Vince got up from the couch placing his hand in the small of his back, moving sluggishly towards the bathroom, dragging one leg behind him. Ovasta chuckled, knowing his movements were exaggerated.

In a few moments, Vince emerged from the bathroom and stood in front of her with his hands behind his back and his legs spread about one foot apart. Peering down at her with burrowed eyebrows. He looked angry.

"What's wrong?" queried Ovasta. Startled by his sudden change in mood. She sat up on the couch.

"I found *this* in the cabinet behind the Tylenol." Vince pulled his arm from behind his back exposing a clear glass medicine bottle. "Please explain why you have Rohypnol in your home. Something that is not only illegal in the United

States but is also used as a date rape drug. How were you even able to purchase this?"

Ovasta's heart began to race once she saw the bottle in his hand. The bottle she thought she'd tossed out on garbage day over a month ago. "I-I-I can explain." Her face felt like it was on fire, ignited by Vince's glower. He had always viewed her from a place of love. Even when he was angry. But now all she saw was disdain in his eyes.

"I am waiting." His voice rumbled like thunder.

"Vince, I was so upset that the police dropped the case. I took matters into my own hands." She put her head down unable to bear his glare. Tears ran down her cheeks.

"Look at me and tell me what you did," Vince spoke through clenched teeth. Ovasta glanced up at him. Her eyes were so tear-filled her vision was blurred. "I went to Joseph Stacolli's party looking for the security man in the newspaper article. I couldn't find him but I did see one of the other men who forced the young man to assault me. I put the drug in his drink and led him out into the parking lot. Once he passed out I kicked him. Twice. I picked up something to kill him with but I couldn't. All I could think of was you. Vince, you have to believe me." Ovasta began to wail. She jumped up from the couch attempting to grasp Vince.

At first, he embraced her. She could feel his body trembling. Something she had never felt before. It broke her heart to know she had caused him pain. Slowly, he pulled away from her.

"I can't do this right now. I have to leave. I need to process this. This is all too much. Do you know what type of position you have placed me in?" He walked over to the front door putting on his boots, hat, and coat.

"Please don't leave, Vince. Can we talk about it?" Her voice was weary.

"No. I'll see you later. It's best that I leave right now." He put on his gloves and turned the doorknob. His eyes shifted for a moment as he peered at Ovasta with reddened eyes. "Did this happen right before Christmas?"

"Yes," Ovasta admitted in a whisper.

"What was the man's name?"

"Vince, I don't see why that matters? It's behind me now, and I know my actions were wrong. I hope you can find it in your heart to forgive me."

"What was his name?" demanded Vince through gritted teeth.

"His last name is Stokes," Ovasta mumbled. "I never got his first name."

"There was a man named Stokes in the ER around that time. I'm sure it was the same man. I recognized the gentleman who rode with him in the ambulance from the newspaper article. The man you told police took part in the assault. Riya and I both saw him that day. We didn't want to tell you he was even in the hospital because I didn't want to bring up any bad memories. You seemed to be doing so much better."

"So you know I didn't really harm him," she said, relieved. Vince grimaced, his nostrils flared.

"Stokes died, Ovasta." He spoke flatly.

A frigid chill permeated through her body. "What? No,

it can't be true." She fell face-down on the floor, sobbing hysterically.

"His injuries didn't kill him. The Rohypnol in his system didn't kill him. Hypothermia did. He froze to death. Remember how cold it was last month? If you didn't want him to die, why didn't you call 911? I thought it was some random act. I never imagined it was you!" Vince's fists were clenched, his body stiff as a board, his eyes now bloodshot.

"I-I-I asked someone to call," she stuttered.

"Someone like who? You had an accomplice! I'm not sure what's going on here but I can't listen to this anymore. I'm starting to believe you're not telling me the whole truth. When we were talking only seconds ago, you never mentioned anyone else was even there."

"It was Junnie. There young man who was forced on me. He came out right after I decided to leave."

"Junnie. How do you know what his name is? You had a conversation with him? This story isn't adding up. Had you met him before the Director's Ball?"

"No. I'd never seen any of them ever before. I swear. Have you ever known me to lie to you in the past? Why would I lie now?"

"I can't answer that question. But I do know that because of your actions, a man is dead. That is not the behavior of the woman I have grown to love." Vince sighed. "I have to get out of here and clear my head. I hope you don't mind that I'm taking your car since you've blocked me in the driveway."

"Vince . . ." Ovasta didn't know what to say.

"There's something I never told you about the night you were assaulted." His eyes were still angry, but his voice was soft. "Remember when I got called away on an emergency on the day of the dinner. When I got to the hospital, there was no emergency and they didn't even have record of anyone calling me. I never mentioned it to you in light of all the other things that happened. I thought it was a hoax and seemed insignificant at the time in light of what happened with you. But, now I wonder if your attack was planned. I feel guilty for leaving you. I should have been there to protect you. I can't protect you from causing a man's death, Ovasta." The anger returned to his voice. "As a physician, I must report you for having illegal drugs in your home or unwittingly become an accomplice as well. Unfortunately, for you, I have a conscience. I don't want to be around you right now."

"Vince, please don't leave. I love you."

"Sometimes love isn't enough." Vince opened the door, darting out into the hallway.

This can't be happening. It can't be. Disbelief, like a hazy mist, clouded her mind.

She lay prostrate on the floor feely dizzy and overwhelmed with grief and pain. Not knowing what to do. Two kicks to the midsection didn't kill Stokes. The cold did. Junnie did.

A monstrous blast jerked her out of her reverie. She whipped her head around as it shook the building's foundation. Major began to howl as he ran toward her.

What in the world was that? Ovasta ran and unlocked the doors to her patio, sliding them open.

"Oh, my God!" She screamed at the top of her lungs as she saw her car up in flames. Black smoke billowed from the car and the wind carried it away from the house. For a moment, she stood there frozen in disbelief. As the flames consumed her car, coldness encamped her body. The car's hood had blown off and was now right side down in the middle of the street. Pieces everywhere. She dashed from one side of the patio to the other in search of Vince. Hoping to see him arise from the ashes.

Should she yell out to him? Call his name? She opened her mouth to no avail. Her throat felt like it had been gripped by a vice. Finally, words escaped her vocal cords like an animal being freed from a trap.

Frantic, she picked up the phone, hands shaking as she dialed 911.

"911. What's your emergency?" said the female voice on the other end of the phone.

"There's been an explosion and I can't find my fiancé!"

She gave the operator her address. Within minutes, the roar of sirens could be heard from a distance. Flashing lights permeated the sky temporarily preventing dusk's descent. A multitude of police officers and firefighters rapidly disembarked from their vehicles and surrounded the area. Immediately, police officers forced onlookers to move away from the scene. Ovasta watched in horror as firefighters extinguished the flames from her car.

Still on the patio, she remained inside, panic-stricken. It

was like watching a horror film and being unable to change the channel. A police officer emerged out of the chaos. Shivering and confused, Ovasta ran and opened the front door before he could knock, studying him carefully.

"Hello, ma'am. I'm officer Howard Clintons. Are you the owner of the burning vehicle?" Soft-spoken, his voice provided a brief respite for her prickly nerves.

"Yes, I'm Ovasta Kaiser, would you like to come in?" her voice cracked as she fought away the tears.

Motionless, Officer Clintons stood there staring. His dark-brown eyes focused on Major. "I would like to come in, ma'am, but not until you put the dog away."

"Okay," she replied weakly.

Major followed her to the bathroom where she locked him inside. Her buckling knees barely carried her back to meet Clintons. He stepped inside after she beckoned to him. Having never made it to the front door, she fell down on the couch, her head reeling.

Officer Clintons closed the door behind him, cutting off the cold air and smoke.

"Do you need an ambulance, ma'am? You appear pale and have an unsteady gait," he suggested while eyeing her as she plopped down.

"No. I'll be alright. Please have a seat."

He sat down, pulling a notepad and pen out of his front pocket. "I need to ask you a few questions concerning this incident. First of all, who was operating the car at the time of the explosion?"

Ovasta's head dropped like someone had hit it from

behind. For a moment, she was silent. "My fiancé, Dr. Vince Parker."

"I'll need all the information you can give me about him, including his next of kin. If you can give me anything with his DNA on it, we'd like to use it to confirm he was actually in the car."

"We recently came back from visiting his parents. His suitcase is over there. There's a toothbrush inside as well as some other items." Ovasta lifelessly pointed to Vince's suitcase in the corner of the room.

"Ma'am, I have to tell you that from my past experiences with these types of explosions, it may well be that your car was rigged to explode as soon as the key turned in the ignition. Is there anyone you can think of who would want to harm you? After all, you did say it was your car, correct?"

Ovasta felt like she had just received a blow to the head. "I have no idea who wants to harm me. I don't know. I can't think right now," she cried, cupping her hands over her face. Her heart felt as if were trapped in a vice. Her head, spinning.

"Miss Kaiser, is there someone you can call? I really don't think you should be alone tonight."

Ovasta lifted up her head. Her eyes red and swollen. Clintons' brown eyes merged with hers.

"Oh, God, how could I have forgotten to call Riya? She's my best friend. I know she'll come."

"I'll wait with you until she gets here. In the meantime, I must inform you that we'll have to tow your car to the station. I'll send you pictures and a police report for insurance purposes."

Ovasta picked up her cell phone, weeping. "Riya . . . something terrible has happened."

TWELVE

U sing DNA from Vince's toothbrush as well as from his parents, forensic evidence confirmed that the remains in Ovasta's car were that of Vince Parker. A memorial service was held in his honor about two weeks following the explosion at the same church where Ovasta had gone to confession right before last Christmas.

A large picture of Vince stood on an easel in front of the high altar surrounded by flowers and three-tiered candelabras on each side. The earthy odor of incense ascended upward dissipating into the building's stone walls. Doctors and medical professionals from across the country came to pay homage to their trusted colleague and friend. Officer Clintons, dressed in a black suit and tie, stood in the back of the church watching for clues or any type of suspicious activity, as the car bombing investigation was ongoing.

Ovasta, wearing a black pill box hat and skirt suit, sat in the front row alongside Vince's parents who had flown in for the service. As mourners passed by to pay their respects, Ovasta felt their whispers crawling underneath her skin as they discussed the unusual circumstances of his demise.

Condemned and ashamed, she fixed her gaze on the stately picturesque building. The priest's words, which were spoken to her during her confessional last year, haunted her as she focused on the stained-glass window with an etching of Mary holding baby Jesus. *But vengeance is God's job, He will repay. When you try to do it yourself, something always goes wrong.* Those words "something always goes wrong" seemed to be an understatement. Vince was dead.

Although she didn't tell the police, Ovasta was almost certain who was behind the car bomb. Williams. Somehow he'd figured she drugged Stokes. He probably assumed she left Stokes' body so he would freeze to death. Whatever the case, Ovasta decided that Williams would pay. Jones would pay. They all would. Just as the flames had consumed her car destroying all but fragments of Vince's body, rage engulfed her mind leaving minuscule pieces of her soul. While the priest concluded the eulogy, Ovasta's body stiffened in the pew as hatred crept through her veins, inevitably cutting off all corridors to her heart.

After the service, Vince's parents went to the hospital where a small reception was being held in his honor. Ovasta opted not to go. It was hard enough facing everyone at the memorial service. She couldn't bear to face them again. Later that evening, Ovasta taxied Vince's parents to the airport in a car she'd been renting for the past couple of weeks.

For the first ten minutes of the ride, there was a heavy silence in the car. Then Mrs. Parker spoke. "If you find out any news concerning Vince, you'll tell us, won't you?" she queried, her small voice emanating from the back seat of the car.

"Yes, Ovasta, we have a right to know what happened to our son," bellowed Mr. Parker from the passenger's seat. He turned his face towards Ovasta. She could see his eyes were bloodshot. We want you to tell us everything you know. It was your car that exploded. Not his. What have you done? Vince didn't deserve this." His words were mixed with anger and grief.

Tears streamed down Ovasta's face. It was really hard knowing that Vince's parents seem to be blaming her for his death. "Honestly, I have no idea what happened. You both know how much I loved your son. Nothing would make me happier than to bring whoever did this to justice. You also have Officer Clintons' phone number. I'm sure he'd be more than happy to give you any updates. He seems to be extremely dedicated."

"Yes, he did seem like such a nice young man. We'll definitely keep up with him. But we also want to hear from you when you're ready to talk. I can always tell when someone is holding something back." Mr. Parker's voice trailed off.

Ovasta could see from that rear view mirror that Mrs. Parker stared blankly out of the car window as the barren trees swayed gently across the gloomy sky.

When they arrived at the airport, Mr. Parker unloaded the luggage from the trunk, his wavy hair and large stature reminiscent of Vince. Ovasta hugged Mrs. Parker goodbye. Mr. Parker stood coldly at a distance only giving her a halfhearted wave. Ovasta pulled away from the terminal quickly to head home assuming she'd never see them again. Her phone rang as she was getting off the exit towards her house.

"Vee, how are you doing?" asked Riya sincerely.

"This is one of the worst days I've ever had. I just dropped Vincent's parents off at the airport. They are devastated."

"Of course, they are. Who expects to lose their child? I can't imagine what they're going through. I didn't even know what to say to them." Riya paused for about three seconds. "Vee, are you going to tell me what really happened? With all that's been going on, I didn't want to push the issue. But I want to know. I need to know. Please don't shut me out," she continued. There was fear fused with sorrow in her voice.

Ovasta felt blood rushing to her face. "You sound like Mr. and Mrs. Parker. Believe me, I want to, but I don't think I can. The less you know, the better."

"What does that mean? You make it sound like it's some sort of covert government mission." Riya sounded angry.

"I'm just saying. There are some things I haven't told you."

"That much is obvious. I'm coming over. I don't like the way this conversation is going. I'd rather talk face to face. I'll pick up some food and we can eat," demanded Riya.

"Okay." Ovasta reluctantly agreed. She didn't think it was safe for Riya to know what had happened. Vince found out and he lost his life. She didn't want anything to happen to Riya.

"I'll see you in about an hour," said Riya.

Ovasta hung up the phone as she was pulling into her driveway. It was getting dark but the space where her car had exploded cast a shadowy darkness into the night. Looking at it made her skin crawl. Tears clouded her vision as she put the key in the door of her home. She felt lost. Hopeless. Alone. She thought she and Vince would be doing life together. Now she would be doing life on her own.

Within the hour, Riya arrived with Chinese food in hand. Very little was communicated as Ovasta put plates on the dining room table and Riya pulled those all-too-familiar cartons out of the bag.

"Alright, let's eat," stated Riya as she sat at the table while handing Ovasta some fried rice. Ovasta pasted a smile on her face, taking the container and pouring rice on a paper plate.

Riya's brows burrowed. "Vee, you have to open up and talk about what's going on. I'm feel like if you don't, you may have a nervous breakdown."

"I know you're worried about me. But since there's a police investigation, I don't want you involved."

Riya studied Ovasta. Shaking her head from side to side. "We've spent so much time together over the past two and a half decades. But something is very different. On my way here, I was concerned. Now, I'm worried. It almost sounds like you're trying to tell me you had something to do with this."

Ovasta stopped eating, glaring at Riya. Squinted eyes. Stiffened neck. "Do you think I wanted this to happen? Do you think I wanted Vince to die? You really believe I killed him. No, I did not kill Vince. I loved him. I *still* love him." Ovasta spoke through gritted teeth, putting her head down, breathing heavily.

Riya rushed to her side, kneeling on the floor beside her friend. "Sweetie, please . . . tell me what you've you done," whispered Riya, with panic sliding into her words.

"I can't. Please understand that this whole ordeal has taken me further than I could ever imagine. I did something illegal. I believe that as a result of my actions, Vince is dead." Riya reached up, embracing Ovasta. They cried, overcome with anguish and grief. Riya picked a napkin from off of the table, pulling back Ovasta's hair then wiping away the tears.

"You have to put an end to this. Will you please go to Officer Clintons and tell him what happened?"

No response. Riya stared at Ovasta. Ovasta stared coldly back. Riya's body seem to grow limp like a balloon being deflated once the air has been released. Beads of sweat formed on Riya's face.

"You're not going to talk to Clintons, are you?" asked Riya.

For a moment, Ovasta sat there repeatedly jabbing her plastic fork rhythmically into the fried rice. Silent. Emotionless. She eyed Riya shaking her head no.

"You are right. It is better that I know as little as possible. I can't support your illegal actions. You've decided to let the pain of your past ruin your future. If you want to talk, you know my number. Goodbye, Ovasta."

Ovasta watched as Riya left the house, gathering her coat and boots as quickly possible. Ovasta could hear Riya crying as she closed the door. She knew she'd lost her best friend.

THIRTEEN

It was the second week of March. The last two months had been a struggle for Ovasta. She'd been prescribed medication for the anxiety she felt every time she got in the car. Whenever she put the keys in the ignition, visions of the explosion flooded her mind. It was so real. Sweat poured down her face. Heart palpitations overcame her. She actually swore she could smell smoke. It was getting to the point where she was unable to drive. A trip to a psychiatrist's office was an easy decision. The odd thing was immediately following Vince's death, she felt no reservations about getting into her car. Now, she drove as little as possible and was seeing a mental health professional to help sort through the myriad of emotions.

Also, she'd recently returned home. She and Major had been staying at a hotel for the past month and a half. Beyond the fact that even walking in the driveway past where the car exploded caused her grief, there were still a few news media hovering around looking for a story. Furthermore, she felt unsafe. Were the people responsible for Vince's death still out there waiting to kill her? After all, she was the original target. Or were they satisfied with what they had done? She couldn't be sure. Cameras and a state-of-the-art security system were placed in her home. It was protected. Prayerfully, so was she.

Ovasta decided that she'd no longer live in fear and had slowly begun to resume normal activities. Today, she and Major went outside for an early morning jog. The weather forecaster predicted unseasonably warm weather for the next seven days. The scent of fresh blossoms infiltrated the air. Birds could be heard chirping in the treetops as they went around the block. After approximately an hour, Ovasta made her way back to the house feeling refreshed.

"Come on, boy. Let's get some breakfast. I'm starving. I'll make sure you get plenty of water. It was much warmer than I thought." Major ran over to his bowl, panting in anticipation of his morning meal. Ovasta opened a can of his favorite dog food and mixed it with some kibble which was under the kitchen sink. After putting water on the other side of the bowl, she placed it on the floor just as her phone was ringing. *Who would be calling this early? It is only 6:30 a.m.!*

"Hello, is this Miss Kaiser?" inquired the male voice on the other end of the phone.

"Yes. Hello, Mr. Harding. I thought you said you'd contact me last week."

"Sorry about that. I apologize for the delay. Things took longer than expected and I wanted to provide as much detail as possible. I believe you'll be pleased with the results. I have all the information you requested and then some. You can pick it up anytime today if you'd like."

"I'll meet you before I go to work. Will you be there around eight thirty?"

"I sure will. See you then."

"See you."

Ovasta got into the shower preparing for a long eventful day, then left her townhouse in her new black BMW with silver Beyern Multi wheel rims. She drove off listening to meditation CD's to calm her nerves, first stopping at the Sterling Building as it was only a few blocks away from work. The building was old and wooden but had been well kept up. Ovasta entered the glass doors, riding the elevator to the ninth floor. She glided across the marble floor, having long since traded in her Pradas for Hush Puppies. At the end of the hallway was Suite 921, Harding's Private Investigation Services. It was a small, sparsely decorated office. Only two plastic chairs in the reception area and two workers in addition to Harding. Harding was the only one in the office at the time of Ovasta's arrival.

He greeted her at the door. "Hello, Miss Kaiser, come on in." Harding was much shorter than Ovasta only reaching her at chin level. He appeared to be about sixty years old, with a head full of gray and white hair. She followed him into his office and sat down in the fabric chair across from his desk.

"Here's the information you requested." He slid a large manila folder across the desk with his short stubby hands.

"Thank you." Ovasta picked up the folder, glancing

inside. "I'll look it over more thoroughly when I get home from work," she continued.

Harding leaned forward, his oval-shaped eyes alarmed. "Miss Kaiser, as I told you when I took this case, you should be very careful. I was in law enforcement for twenty-five years prior to retiring and becoming a PI. The Stacolli family is very dangerous."

"As I told *you* before, I'm quite aware of the danger involved."

Ovasta's curt response caused Harding to sit backwards in his chair. "Alright. It was just a friendly warning. I've seen many people get harmed and even killed due to their dealings with this family. I want to make sure you know what you're getting into."

Ovasta pushed an envelope across the table ignoring his comments.

Harding picked it up and thumbed through a large wad of money. "This seems like the right amount."

"Then I guess we're done here." Ovasta got up hastily and headed towards the door.

"It's been a pleasure, Miss Kaiser. I wish you luck."

"Thank you. Have a good day." Ovasta strode out of the office and back down the hallway.

After work, Ovasta picked up a salad from a local restaurant then headed home. Once she finished eating and fed Major, she opened her briefcase and grabbed the folder she received from Harding spreading the contents of the folder across her dining room table. In it were the names, addresses, and pictures of all of Stacolli's employees. As promised by Harding, the report was extremely thorough. Ovasta was pleased to find Jones' and Williams' starting times, quitting times, and usual routes traveled to and from the Stacolli home. Additionally, there were city schematics of the compound where the Stacolli family lived, as well as the Stacolli family tree.

A plan was devised after studying all the information. At about 1:00 a.m. the next morning, she dressed from head to toe in all black. Then drove to the highway where Jones traveled every night on his way home from work and pulled her car on the highway shoulder. After turning her hazard lights on, she popped open her car hood, putting her head underneath, pulling a hoodie over her head. Almost immediately, a car pulled in behind hers. The rear lights shone against a white Chevy Malibu. The make and model were wrong. It wasn't Jones. *Keep your cool. Don't panic.*

A male stuck his head out of the window. "Can I help you, ma'am?" queried the deep voice.

"No, thanks. My fiancé should be here in about two minutes."

"Would you like me to wait with you? It's pretty dark out here."

"No thanks. He really is on his way."

"Alright, have it your way."

Ovasta breathed a sigh of relief as the Malibu pulled

away. She began pacing back and forth in front of the car, wondering if Harding's information was correct.

A few minutes later, another set of headlights pulled in behind her. Peering around the hood sideways, she could see it was Jones' car. A restored 1970 gold Chevy Chevelle SS 454. He cautiously ambled towards her with his hand in his inner coat jacket pocket.

"Do you need some help?" he inquired drawing closer to her.

"Yes, I do. My car started making some strange noises so I pulled over to the side. Now it seems like it won't even start back up."

"I'm surprised considering the kind of car it is. Let me take a look-see."

Ovasta handed Jones a flashlight and turned her head quickly so he couldn't get a good look at her. He moved the flashlight around, searching for anything out of place.

"I don't see anything. Why don't you try to start it? Maybe I can hear what's going on?"

"Will do. Let me get the key out of my pocket." Ovasta pulled a syringe out of her pocket, swiftly thrusting it into his neck. Pushing in the liquid contents as hard as she could. Jones grabbed her hand, but before he could jerk the needle away his hand became limp. His widened eyes glared at her.

"*You*," his fleeting voice barely able to push out the words as he collapsed in front of her car.

"Yes, me," she said sarcastically with a smirk on her face while watching him tumble to the ground. She put the car hood down, got in her car putting it in reverse. Slowly, she backed away, avoiding Jones' body. *I don't want any traces of blood or DNA on my car.* She drove off, never looking back.

It was 3 a.m. when she entered her apartment. *I just killed a man. This time on purpose. There's no turning back now.* She stretched herself across the bed contemplating her next move while awaiting daylight. The alarm rang at 5:30. Major was already sitting there, leash in mouth. Ovasta performed her regular routine— morning run, feed Major, take a shower.

While getting dressed, the picture of Vince on her nightstand caught her attention. She picked up the clear frame, stroking her hands deliberately across his face. It was her favorite picture of him. Taken when he'd gone on a mission's trip to Africa where he performed surgeries on the natives. Having not shaved in several weeks, he looked ruggedly handsome standing next to one of the makeshift hospitals in the area. He was so giving of himself to others. He didn't deserve to die. Especially the way he did. Tears dropped on his photo, gradually increasing in volume like a torrential rainstorm. It was March 15th. Her wedding day. It should have been the happiest day of her life. Now she was left with only emptiness, bitterness, abhorrence. She slid the 4x6 out of the side of the frame, kissed it and glided it underneath her T-shirt over her left breast, pressing it down. *Vince, I want you near me 'til the end.*

Deep down, she knew that he wouldn't agree with her actions. His last words rang loudly in her head. *"I have a conscience."* Vince was a good man. Had it not been for

Williams, Ovasta was sure that she and Vince would have been able to talk and work things out. They loved each other deeply. Williams stole their chance for happiness. As good of a man as Vince was, Ovasta wanted to believe that he loved her enough that he would have revenged her death if the cops didn't. Maybe she felt that way to ease her own conscience. Whatever the case, she was all in now, and she was going to make sure that those monsters could not destroy anyone else's life. Ovasta put on some jeans and her tennis shoes, left her apartment and dropped Major off at a kennel. Because she was unsure of her return, she gave them Riya's number as an emergency contact.

In the car, she grabbed the folder which was lying on the passenger side of the front seat and pulled out Joseph Stacolli's photo. His name and address were on it. *1837 Graswood Lane. This is where it all ends. There's nothing left for me here. Everything . . . everyone . . . is gone.* Ovasta felt alone. Like Thelma sans Louise. She let out a big sigh placing her right hand over Vince's picture, over her heart. She put Stacolli's address in the GPS and turned on the radio, blasting "Life is a Highway" through the speakers.

With the window down and a chilly breeze blowing through her black hair, she sped down the highway. Her right hand on the steering wheel and the left pounding the beat on her chest, rocking her head from side to side, shouting out the song's lyrics.

Per the GPS, the distance from Ovasta's home to the Stacolli compound was approximately thirty-eight minutes. Ovasta made it there in twenty and parked on the side of the road about a quarter-mile from the gated entrance. She jumped out of the car and popped her trunk pushing back the spare tire cover. Where a tire should have been, was enough explosives to blow up the entire block.

Ovasta strapped the explosives over her T-shirt like a bulletproof vest overlaying it with a beige London Fog trenchcoat, tying the belt across the front of her body. The detonator already in the coat pocket. According to Harding's report, Williams should be on duty. *I hope Harding was right. If not, I'll have to wing it.*

The trek was filled with apprehension as well as memories of times past. Within less than a year, things had changed more dramatically than she could have ever imagined. The life she envisioned was now a distant memory, like an empty bottle floating across the shores of life.

Up ahead, the guard station could be seen in the far distance. Ovasta decided to pick up the pace as the weight of the explosives had begun to slow her down. Williams spotted her even before she could get to the gate.

"Whoever you are, we don't want any," he said, gruffly yelling through a megaphone out the window of the glass enclosure.

She strode faster in his direction pretending not to hear him.

"Hey, lady, stop right now or I'll have to use force." He slid the door to one side, dropping the megaphone, stepping out, heading towards her. She looked him square in the eye. Head held high. Hands in her pockets.

Finally, he recognized her and grimaced. "You dare

come here after what you've done," he hissed, stopping in his tracks. He pulled back his blazer and snatched the pistol from his side holster, sneering, pointing it at her head. "I'm going to blow your head off and hide the body so no one will ever find it."

Ovasta gave him a sinister laugh surprising even herself. "I'm wearing a bomb, you might not want to do that." A wave of confidence encompassed her, bringing with it the prowess of a lioness.

"You're bluffing." An angry vein forced its way to the top of his forehead.

"Would you like to frisk me?" asked Ovasta in a smooth seductive voice.

He barked. "You think this is a joke! Open your coat... slowly." He moved closer now, beckoning for her to open the coat by swaying the pistol to one side.

She pulled the tie and opened her trench coat, exposing the bomb, quickly reaching back into her pocket to hit the timer before Williams could react. He hopped backwards upon hearing the high-pitched sound, almost dropping the pistol, the digital display in the center of the bomb burning his pupils. Fifteen minutes on the timer.

"Are you out of your mind? What do you want, lady? You're the one who killed Stokes. You started this!"

Ovasta remained stoic while trying to figure out how he could possibly know that and wondering when they would find out about Jones. "What makes you think that?"

Williams shook his head in disgust. "Amateur. There were cameras everywhere. Jones and I saw you on the tape.

We recognized you even with the red wig and glasses. You were at Boss' party. You were the last person to be seen with Stokes. We both promised Boss we'd take care of you."

For a moment, Ovasta lost her train of thought. *How could I have been so stupid?* She took a deep breath redirecting her focus on Williams. "You killed my fiancé, Vince. He was the love of my life. My prince charming. My happily ever after."

Williams had a crooked smile on his face. "Heh. That'll teach him to drive his own car. The bomb was meant for you."

Ovasta cringed inside at the thought that Williams could make a joke out of Vince's death. "You're not worth talking to. I came here to see Mr. Stacolli. Tell him my side of the story. For him, I'll cut the bomb off."

Williams was taken aback. "You're taking a big chance, lady. I'll take you to him but I guarantee it won't do you any good. You'd be better off if I shot you right now." He grabbed the radio from out of the guard post. "Boss, I'm sorry to bother you but I have someone here who wants to see you. It's a code red."

Ovasta heard a brusque voice shriek out of the radio.

"What do I pay you for? Can't you handle anything? This better be worth my time or you'll regret it. Alright, come on. Bring her in."

Williams' large frame shrunk under the weight of Stacolli's words. He led Ovasta to a golf cart hidden behind a wall on the south side of the guard post signaling for her to get in, then he jumped in, keeping his eye on the timer as if staring at it would make it stop. Thirteen minutes on the timer.

Williams drove carelessly across the bleak landscape plowing through stubbles of grass and bloomless bushes as he went. In the center of the compound was a beautiful water fountain with a large statue of a cherub. Ovasta could have enjoyed the view were it not for the circumstances and Williams' driving. Once at the front door, he sprang out of the cart and unlocked it, bolting inside.

"Wait here," he said almost out of breath.

It was the first word he had uttered since scolded by Stacolli. Backwards, Williams trotted away from her eyeing the timer while disappearing into the enormousness of the house. Eleven minutes on the timer.

Ovasta stood there mouth agape as she studied the area. Simple but elegant. *What was that?* Alarmed, Ovasta's head snapped around. Noises and shouting came from one of the rooms. She moved closer to the noise trying to decipher what was being said. Within seconds, Williams came running towards her.

"Come on, move it. Boss wants to see you right now," Williams demanded. Hurriedly, Ovasta followed Williams into what appeared to be a den. Williams went in first and stood on Stacolli's right side, arms crossed, and legs spread at attention reminiscent of the guards at Buckingham Palace. Stacolli was standing in the middle of the floor near a brown recliner, in blue shirt and khakis looking like he was headed to the office.

"You dare disrespect the sanctity of my home coming

here with a bomb." He eyed her chest squinting. "There are nine minutes on the timer. You only have five to explain yourself." He peered at her. Accordion-like creases formed across his forehead.

Although Stacolli's commanding presence could not be ignored, Ovasta was determined not to diminish her stance. He extended his hand towards Williams palm up, never taking his eye off her. Williams pulled the gun out of his holster and handed it to Stacolli who held the gun down at his side.

Ovasta trembled. Her voice shook. "Sir, I know you believe I killed Stokes but I didn't. It was not my fault he froze to death, but I do admit drugging him." Ovasta saw Stacolli's hand with the gun rise slowly towards her and spoke more rapidly.

"I did it to get revenge because Stokes, Jones, and Williams forced your grandson, Junnie, to rape me."

Joseph's nose flared like a raging bull. He turned his attention to Williams.

"Boss, it's not true. Don't believe her," cried Williams.

Ovasta interrupted. Pleading with Stacolli. "You don't have to believe me. Can't you call him? He'll tell you what really happened and confirm that I am telling you the truth."

"You better hope he answers 'cuz you only have three minutes. Williams, dial his number, and put it on speaker," ordered Boss.

Williams retrieved his cell phone out of his blazer and

dialed Junnie. The phone rang once. Ovasta could see his hand twitching.

"Yes, Williams." Junnie sounded irritated.

"Son, its Granddad. I need you to head over here as fast as possible. I have a woman standing in front of me who claims Williams, Jones, and Stokes forced you to have relations with her. Is that true?" The phone was quiet. "Son, did you hear me?" Junnie's tears could be heard through the speaker.

"Yes, Granddad, they did," he mumbled.

Joseph's face morphed into the murderous mobster Harding warned Ovasta about. Perspiration seeped through the underarm section of her trench coat.

"Boss, I can explain. *He* told us to do it. *He* planned the whole thing." Bawling, quivering, Williams pointed past Ovasta.

There was a presence behind her. She was afraid to move. Stacolli pointed the gun at Williams' head and pulled the trigger. Ovasta heard a *pop*. Williams's head jerked backwards. His body tumbled to the floor like a tree chopped down in the forest. The cell phone reaching the ground before he did which caused the battery to pop out. Blood gushed out of the wound in his head.

"Oh, my God!" she said under her breath. Stacolli heard her then squinted. She knew she was next.

"He knew better than to harm my family. You're in luck. I've decided to give you Williams' four minutes. He doesn't need them anymore." He smiled at Ovasta. His cool, calm demeanor unnerved her. Those vacant eyes made her body limp. She felt like she was going to void the contents of her stomach.

"Come on out. I need you to explain yourself." Stacolli was peering around her.

Without moving her head, she attempted to glance behind her. A tall, lean figure ambled past her. Her mouth dropped, her eyes widened, and her pulse raced when she saw him. *Phillip!* She was unable to speak. It was as someone had their hand around her throat, choking the life out.

"Hello, Ovasta." Phillip gave her a blank stare. Stunned, her limbs started to ache. Out of the corner of her eye, she noticed Stacolli looking at her.

"I see you've met my son," said Stacolli.

Ovasta's heart began to pound so intensely, she thought it would inadvertently set off the explosives. "S-s-son?" she stuttered.

Phillip replied. "Yes. Remember when I told you I found out who my dad was. Well, let me introduce you to my father, Joseph Stacolli. I'm proud to be a part of this family. They've stood by me these past couple of years like no one else ever has. Certainty not you or even my own wife. I heard people wondered why my wife left me. She claimed she didn't want to be involved with the Stacolli's because they had been linked to too many crimes. The more I hung out with them, the less she wanted to be around. I tried to explain to her that they hadn't ever been convicted of anything but she decided to leave. I have no idea where she is and haven't heard from her since. Actually, last year I tried to find her and reconnect but to no avail. Anyway, it doesn't matter now. She's not my family. They are." Phillip turned to Boss. "This is Ovasta Kaiser. She's the president of the board of directors at the hospital."

Boss frowned. "Wait a minute. Please tell me that is not what this is about? Your ego, your jealousy. 'Cuz she was elected and not you? I told you when you called me that day you still had us. What more do you need?" Stacolli's top lip curved upwards as he ranted, exposing his gapped teeth.

Junnie rushed in as Stacolli was talking, wrapping his arms around his grandad's midsection. All the while, looking down at Williams' dead body.

Boss hugged Junnie. "Tell me what happened?"

"Granddad, I was afraid to say anything about what happened that night because Williams kept threatening me. Saying that if I told what they did he had information that would put you and my dad in jail. But, yes, they forced me to touch her. I didn't want to. Williams said it was because I was gay and that they wanted to make a man out of me. Junnie started to cry while placing his head in his grandfather's chest."

"Did you know about this?" Stacolli questioned Phillip. A sinister look donned his face.

"Yes. It was Patrick, John, and Carl's idea. We went to lunch one day and they told me about their plans. I had nothing to do with it," answered Phillip, his voice quivering.

"Then how did this woman get involved? Why would Patrick pick her?" asked Stacolli, his eyes filled with anger.

Phillip began to stutter. "B-b-boss, like Junnie said, they told me they were trying to make a man out of him."

"Imbecile, he's not a man. He's sixteen years old and shouldn't be having relations with anyone! At thirteen, he took the oath of chastity. You made him break that oath! It's against God and our religious upbringing."

Junnie let go of Boss who began to pace the floor swinging the gun back and forth. With each step, his midsection jiggled. "Stella never wanted you around. You've always been a thorn in her side. The car accident that your mother died in was no accident at all. I've had several indiscretions over the years. They all suffered the same fate." He stopped pacing. Ovasta saw him glaring at Phillips's tear-sodden face when he heard his mother's death was not an accident. Stacolli appeared indifferent, and resumed talking, pacing. "I begged Stella to spare you. She did it because she loves me. Everything she's done was because she loved me. For the record, the reason you can't find your ex-wife is because she's dead. She left town spreading our family secrets. Secrets I bet you told her. Williams disposed of her quietly. Made it look like an accident." He paused for a moment. "You know what. I should have let Stella kill you when she wanted to. But she'll be happy to know I did it myself."

Phillip got down on his knees in front of Stacolli with his palms together like he was praying.

"Boss, please. *Dad*. . . I'm begging you, don't shoot."

"I'm not your dad. You're the mistake I made while I was messing around with your mother. God rest her soul." Stacolli genuflected with the gun in his hand. Pointing it downward, he shot Phillip in the head.

"Oh, Phillip!" Ovasta cried, as he dropped on the floor

in front of the couch, his blood-splattered glasses still secured on his face. Horror engulfed her. This was worse than all of her nightmares combined. Junnie didn't seem as affected as Ovasta thought he should be. He was probably used to this kind of retribution. She knew that it was no accident that Stokes was left in the cold to die.

Stacolli studied her. "Miss, for the record I wouldn't believe him. He's quick to tell a lie. He was definitely involved. There are thirty seconds on the clock. Are you going to stop it?" Ovasta's eyes shifted from Junnie to Stacolli, then back to Junnie. She couldn't read Stacolli's poker face but had seen Junnie in action. She believed the instant she stopped the timer, she'd be dead. Unsure, she hit four buttons on the front of her chest. The timer made a high-pitched noise. Ten minutes added. Enough time for her to get out of harm's way.

"Heh. You're smarter than I thought. Junnie, please escort this woman out of my house. We'll talk later."

"Yes, sir."

Junnie moved towards the den's entrance, never looking at Ovasta. She couldn't believe how nonchalant he was about the whole ordeal. He never flinched when he saw Williams' dead body or Phillip being shot in the head. Briskly, he led her to the front door.

"Isn't there a back way out of here? One that goes underground to the street." Junnie squinted his eyes at her question. "How could you possibly know that?"

"I did my homework. I'd like to head out the back way if I could."

He shook his head at her, rolling his eyes in an upward motion. "Haven't you figured it out? It doesn't matter which way you leave. You've witnessed way too much. The only reason you're leaving right now is because you have a bomb attached to your chest. Eventually, Granddad will find you and then, you're dead."

Ovasta's body ached with terror. The coldness in his voice almost caused her heart to stop beating. Once again she was caught off guard by his callousness. He took her through the dining area, out of the sliding glass doors to the back yard. There was a structure which looked like a garage where the grass met the pavement.

"If you open that door, there are steps going down leading to a tunnel. At the end of the tunnel, there are stairs going upward. Push the door open. It is covered over by grass so as not to be seen from the street. Once out, you'll be facing north," said Junnie, his blank stare triggering a chill down her spine.

"Thank you. Tell me, what happened to the young man who was so sorry about being made to assault me?"

"This from the woman with the bomb attached to her. I could ask you the same question. You better leave before Granddad changes his mind."

Ovasta held her head down and turned away from him. After pulling the thin metal handle on the door, she hopped down the seven steps and bolted as fast as her shoes could take her, dropping her sweat-stained trench coat along the way, the cobwebs attaching themselves to her body. She fell once, tearing a hole in her jeans, the adrenaline keeping her from feeling any pain. She picked herself up and kept running. The barely-lit tunnel seemed endless. Finally, she spotted the stairs, sprinted upwards, and then pushed the door open, moving the foliage out of the way. She glanced at the timer. It only took eight minutes. It seemed like forever. Ovasta removed the vest with thirty seconds on the clock. She threw it down the steps, gave a sinister smile, and shut the door placing the shrubbery back over the exit. By the time she was done, the timer reached zero seconds. No explosion.

She hurried down the street and jumped on a public bus which was headed downtown. After boarding, she rode the bus approximately three minutes before sliding her hand on the left side of her body where she had a tiny holster containing another detonator. Junnie's words echoed in her mind as she pushed it. *Eventually, Granddad will find you and then, you're dead.* Her car, which was still parked down the road from the Stacolli house, had a bomb underneath the bottom of it. Within ten seconds, it blew up along with half the compound. The explosion could be heard for miles. People on the bus ran towards the back, staring out the windows, trying to figure out what was going on. The bus driver called the dispatcher who notified local law enforcement. Flames and smoke shot out in the air seeping into the bus. Ovasta sat quietly in her seat, never looking back.

FOURTEEN

Immediately following the explosion, news media across the country covered the story. Joseph Stacolli, James Williams, Phillip Michaels, and Ovasta Kaiser were all declared dead as a result of video surveillance provided by Ralph Stacolli Sr., who was out with his mother at the time of the incident. Footage showed all four entering the home but never exiting prior to the explosion. Junnie managed to survive the blast but was in critical condition. The injuries to his face, legs, and arms would require multiple surgeries during the upcoming months. Ovasta watched the media frenzy on the television of her Motel Six hotel room. Video coverage showed the Stacolli compound. Debris was everywhere. Police with dogs, FBI, and other first responders combed through the rubbish wearing face masks. Officer Clintons was interviewed at the scene and asked if he believed the explosion which killed Vince Parker was connected to this explosion. He informed reporters that any connection was premature and he was unable to discuss the case at this time. He deferred all comments to the lead FBI agent and walked away from reporter.

Before the agent was interviewed, a wide view of the landscape was shown. Ovasta wept over the devastation she had caused. Making her consider turning herself in. However, she didn't feel as if it would do any good. She could never give back what she had taken or what she had lost.

On one occasion, her home was shown surrounded by police tape and swarming with reporters all trying to piece together what really happened. News stories ranged from Ovasta being a scorned mistress of Stacolli to her being hired as a hitman by the Garmini family. One reporter attempted to interview Riya about what happened. Seeing Riya dodging reporters on television made Ovasta realize she owed her friend an explanation of everything that had occurred over the past few weeks.

At six o'clock the next Sunday morning, Ovasta put on her red wig, a black overcoat, and dark sunglasses. Since Riya was now caring for Major, Ovasta went to the park near Riya's home hoping to catch them on a morning run. She sat on a wooden bench just inside the park's entrance. Waiting. By 6:30, she saw a twenty-something-year-old man in biker shorts and a sweatshirt run past her faster than a cheetah on the hunt. Other than the lone runner, the streets were fairly quiet. Birds could be heard chirping in the barren trees announcing morning. Dew covered the freshly-sprouted grass as there had been a rainstorm the night before. At 7:00 a.m., the sun was beginning to rise.

Ovasta decided to head back to her motel and attempt to see Riya another day. She got up, moving leisurely towards the park entrance. She heard a dog barking when she got to the sidewalk. Major. Ovasta kept her eye on him as they got closer, wondering when he would pick up her scent. At around fifty feet away, he started barking frantically, jerking away from Riya's grip.

"Major, what's wrong, boy?" shouted Riya while pulling on his leash.

"Major, come on, boy!" cried Ovasta, kneeling to the ground extending her arms.

"Vee, oh, my God, is that you? Is it really you?" asked Riya as she recognized the voice. She let Major's leash go. He lunged forward, jumping on Ovasta, almost knocking her over. Excitedly, she hugged him and rubbed his fur. Finally, Riya caught up. "Vee, I ...I thought you were dead." Riya cried while opening her arms towards Ovasta. They embraced tightly while Major hopped up and down at their feet. Instantly, Riya shuddered away from her. Loosening her grip and dropping her arms almost as quickly as she embraced her. Her facial expression transformed from happy to horrified. "Did you blow up all of those people? Did you kill Phillip?"

"No. Phillip and Williams were already dead when the explosive went off. Stacolli killed them. Phillip was responsible for the rape. He set up the whole thing because he was jealous I was elected over him. Believe it or not, I found out that he was Stacolli's son."

"What! I can't believe it. That wasn't in the newspaper. I couldn't figure out what in the world he was doing there. Actually, I was unsure why you were there." Riya hesitated, staring at Ovasta. "You didn't kill Phillip, but you did kill Stacolli and injure his grandson. Is that correct?" she continued.

"Yes. I am responsible. I blew up the compound because they were responsible for Vince's death and it was either kill or be killed. They were never going to let me live. I'm one hundred percent sure of it."

Riya walked over and sat on a nearby bench. She leaned forward and cupped her hands over her face. Rocking back and forth. Ovasta stared at her friend rubbing her back but not knowing what to say next.

Finally, Riya spoke. "This is like a bad dream. A nightmare. How did you make it out alive?"

"I did my research and found out that there was an underground tunnel at the Stacolli home. That's why the video footage doesn't show me leaving since I exited from underground. They only let me leave because I had a bomb on my chest. The reality was it was never set to detonate. The timer was a fake. The real bomb was attached to my car. As soon as I got far enough away, I hit the switch."

Riya shook her head in disbelief. "What are you going to do now?"

"You know I can't stay here. I'll be leaving the country in the next couple of days. Take care of yourself and Major."

Riya looked at her with reddened eyes. "I may never see you again, but don't go through the rest of your life living in anger, feeding it. Anger is never satisfied. It will keep wanting more."

"I'll remember you said that. Goodbye, Riya."

Briefly, they embraced. Ovasta wondered if she'd ever see her again. If she'd ever have a better friend than Riya.

"Goodbye, Ovasta," said Riya somewhat angrily as their embrace ended. Riya grabbed Major and ran into the park's entrance. Ovasta went in the opposite direction towards the motel. She could hear Riya crying and Major whimpering as they left and moved away as quickly as their cries penetrated her heart.

FIFTEEN

A warm breeze blew across the white sand beaches of Jamaica. The weather and stunning scenery made it the perfect location for a new home. Ovasta was lying on a beach chair under a large umbrella wearing a red-and-white bikini, dark sunglasses, and a large hat which covered her now short blond hair. Next to her was Major in his own beach chair with an umbrella. It had been over a year since she left the United States.

"Let's go, Major, I have to go to work," she said to her furry friend, thinking how she couldn't bear to leave him behind. About a month after the explosion, Riya met her at the airport with Major in tow right before she flew to Jamaica.

Thankfully, all of that was behind her. She picked a towel up from the sand and wrapped it around herself, and jogged about a fourth of a mile across the beach to the villa she purchased using the money from Vince's insurance policy and her savings. Her new home reminiscent of her former one.

After a quick shower to wash away the sand, she headed

to work in a small office building only a ten-minute drive from her home. Clad in a blue-and-white floral sundress and flip flops, she entered the four-story brick building where she took the elevator to the third floor.

"Hello, ma'am. How are things going today?" said her receptionist Priscilla Stern as she entered the Rape Crisis Center. Ms. Stern was a fifty-five-year-old Jamaican woman with beautiful bronze skin and hazel brown eyes housed by small rectangular-shaped glasses.

"Everything is great!"

"I took the liberty of letting your first patient go into your office since you were running a little late. I gave her a cup of tea. She seems terribly upset."

"I'm sure she is. That's why I'm here." Ovasta entered her office. The sage green walls donned two frames, one containing a license in Clinical Counseling, the other a doctorate degree in social work. Both awarded to "Ovasta Parker." On Ovasta's desk was the picture of Vince which had been on her nightstand when she lived in the States.

The smell of orange spice tea seeped out of the red, white, and green mug on a circular coffee table. Next to it was a brown leather couch where the patient was crying into her hands.

"Dr. Parker, I'm so glad to see you. I've had the worst week ever. I don't know how to deal with the pain and anger I feel. Its eating me alive," cried the twenty-something Jamaican woman with a slim build and cornrowed hair.

"Please call me Vee." Ovasta turned towards the door

away from the client. A crooked smile covered her face. Her eyebrows knit together. Her voice deepened.

"I understand the anger you feel. You have to learn how to express your anger. I assure you, I can help you with that." With a wide swing of her right arm, she slammed the red office door shut.